DRAGON FORCE
DEVOURER'S ATTACK

Also by Katie and Kevin Tsang

Dragon Realm Books

Dragon Mountain

Dragon Legend

Dragon City

Sam Wu Is Not Afraid Books

Sam Wu Is Not Afraid of Ghosts

Sam Wu Is Not Afraid of Sharks

Sam Wu Is Not Afraid of the Dark

Sam Wu Is Not Afraid of Spiders

DRAGON FORCE

DEVOURER'S ATTACK

BOOK TWO

KATIE & KEVIN TSANG

Simon & Schuster Books for Young Readers

New York   Amsterdam/Antwerp   London   Toronto
Sydney/Melbourne   New Delhi

If you purchased this book without a cover, you should be aware that this book is stolen property. It was reported as "unsold and destroyed" to the publisher, and neither the author nor the publisher has received any payment for this "stripped book."

SIMON & SCHUSTER BOOKS FOR YOUNG READERS
An imprint of Simon & Schuster Children's Publishing Division
1230 Avenue of the Americas, New York, New York 10020
For more than 100 years, Simon & Schuster has championed authors and the stories they create. By respecting the copyright of an author's intellectual property, you enable Simon & Schuster and the author to continue publishing exceptional books for years to come. We thank you for supporting the author's copyright by purchasing an authorized edition of this book.
No amount of this book may be reproduced or stored in any format, nor may it be uploaded to any website, database, language-learning model, or other repository, retrieval, or artificial intelligence system without express permission. All rights reserved. Inquiries may be directed to Simon & Schuster, 1230 Avenue of the Americas, New York, NY 10020 or permissions@simonandschuster.com.
This book is a work of fiction. Any references to historical events, real people, or real places are used fictitiously. Other names, characters, places, and events are products of the author's imagination, and any resemblance to actual events or places or persons, living or dead, is entirely coincidental.
Text © 2024 by Katie Tsang and Kevin Tsang
Cover illustration © 2024 by Petur Antonsson
Interior illustration and map © 2024 by Petur Antonsson
All rights reserved, including the right of reproduction in whole or in part in any form.
SIMON & SCHUSTER BOOKS FOR YOUNG READERS
and related marks are trademarks of Simon & Schuster, LLC.
For information about special discounts for bulk purchases, please contact Simon & Schuster Special Sales at 1-866-506-1949 or business@simonandschuster.com.
Simon & Schuster strongly believes in freedom of expression and stands against censorship in all its forms. For more information, visit BooksBelong.com.
The Simon & Schuster Speakers Bureau can bring authors to your live event.
For more information or to book an event, contact the Simon & Schuster Speakers Bureau at 1-866-248-3049 or visit our website at www.simonspeakers.com.
Also available in a Simon & Schuster Books for Young Readers hardcover edition
The text for this book was set in Adobe Garamond Pro.
The illustrations for this book were rendered digitally.
Manufactured in the United States of America
0525 BID
First Simon & Schuster Books for Young Readers paperback edition June 2025
2 4 6 8 10 9 7 5 3 1
Library of Congress Cataloging-in-Publication Data
Names: Tsang, Katie, 1987- author. | Tsang, Kevin, author.
Title: Devourer's attack / Katie & Kevin Tsang.
Description: First Simon & Schuster Books for Young Readers hardcover edition. | New York: Simon & Schuster Books for Young Readers, 2025. | Series: Dragon force; book 2 | Audience term: Preteens | Audience: Ages 8–12. | Audience: Grades 4–6. | Summary: "Siblings Lance and Zoe must save their Camp Claw mentors from a dangerous, power-hungry creature" —Provided by publisher.
Identifiers: LCCN 2024053377 (print) | LCCN 2024053378 (ebook) | ISBN 9781665962544 (hardcover) | ISBN 9781665962537 (paperback) | ISBN 9781665962551 (ebook)
Subjects: CYAC: Siblings—Fiction. | Dragons—Fiction. | Magic—Fiction. | Human-animal relationships—Fiction. | Fantasy. | LCGFT: Fantasy fiction. | Novels.
Classification: LCC PZ7.1.T768 De 2025 (print) | LCC PZ7.1.T768 (ebook) | DDC [Fic]—dc23
LC record available at https://lccn.loc.gov/2024053377
LC ebook record available at https://lccn.loc.gov/2024053378
ISBN 9781665962544 (hc)
ISBN 9781665962537 (pbk)
ISBN 9781665962551 (ebook)

*To Rachel Denwood, for making all
our dragon dreams come true*

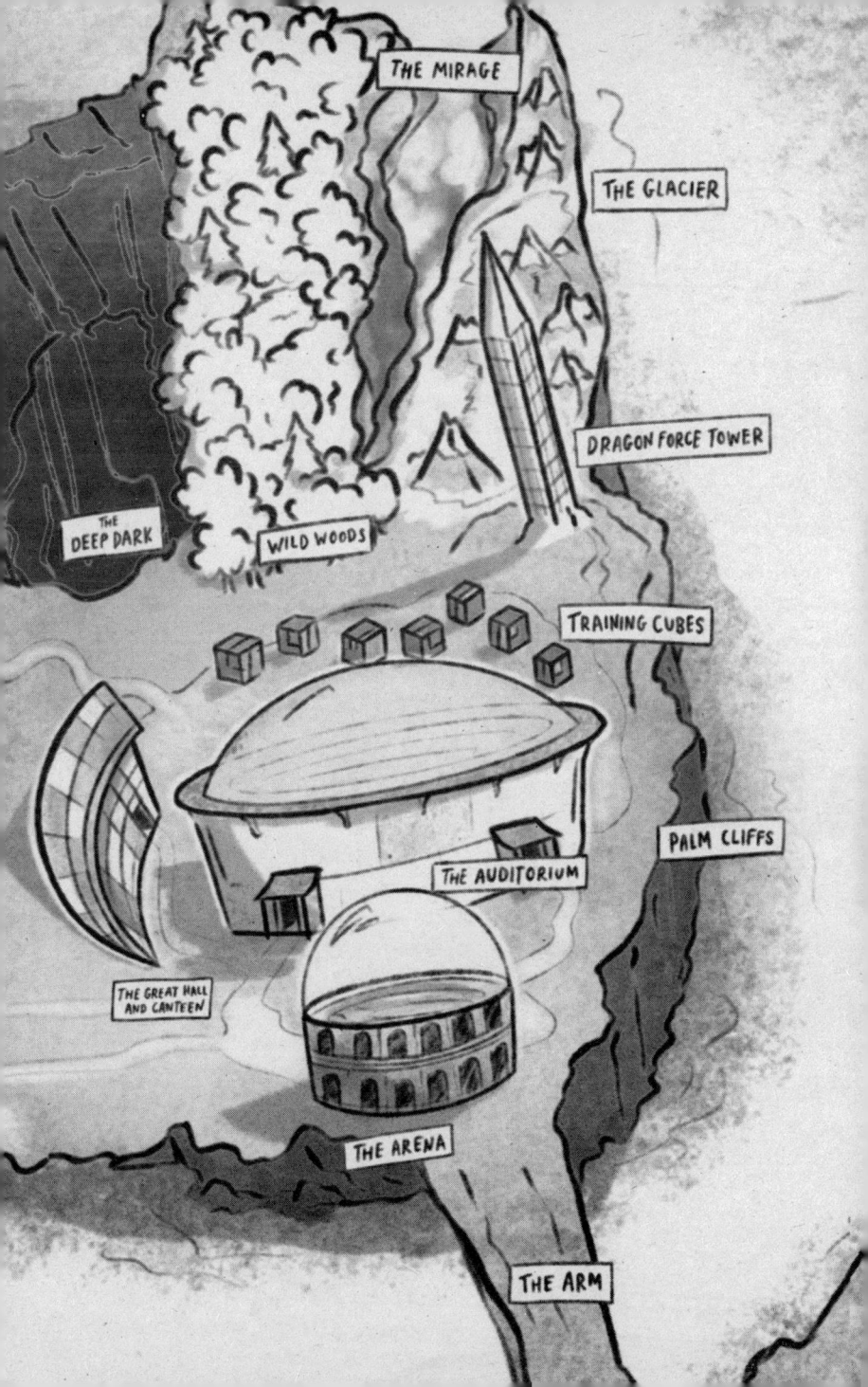

The Shadow in the Sky

There is a shadow in the sky.

At first glance, it looks like a dark cloud, but no. It is a long shadow of something approaching.

Of something from beyond the sky.

Of something that is coming.

The shadow is there, day and night, and it is growing and spreading. The stars that watch it shudder, for they know that now there is no stopping it.

High in the sky there is a hidden den. Made of bone and ice, it twists and turns, and should not stay afloat, but it is crackling with magic. With power.

A swirling cloud of dust and fumes protects the

maze. Poison permeates the air, and every breath you take leaves you more dazed. The closer you get to the center, the colder it becomes. The coldness, and the confusion, is inescapable.

And what lies in the center . . . ? What is waiting for you in the maze . . . ?

Horrors await. Horrors that will strike such fear into your heart that you will find yourself petrified. And you will join others like yourself. Frozen and floating and trapped. Unable to leave the maze, until the Devourer arrives—but by then, all will be lost.

But even in horror, there is hope.

Among the trapped in the maze are a young man and his dragon, both stripped of power and of movement, but still living, still aware. And they stare not at the rapidly growing shadow in the sky, but at the last thing they saw before the fear took over. They stare at the distant ground below. At a new land, one shaped like a dragon's claw, left empty but for four children and their dragons. The only ones who can save them all.

They are the only hope for those trapped in this hidden den in the sky.

But the shadow is growing, the cold is spreading, and time is running out.

The Devourer is coming.

A Hidden Enemy

Lance Lo stood atop the Volcano, staring at the stars.

His dragon, Infinity, stood next to him, her orange-and-gold wings spread and ready for flight. Both of them were alert and wide awake, even though Lance knew he should be exhausted.

Lance gazed out at Dragon's Claw. The peninsula comprised four distinct claws of land, and three lagoons between—and when you took in everything together as Lance did now, it appeared as a dragon stretching its claws. The Volcano was on one side, where the "thumb" would be, then the Water Jungle, which glowed vibrant colors and was full of a multitude of rare water plants, followed by the Labs, flickering with electricity and thrumming with molecule magic, then the Deep Dark, with its fathomless inky depths, the Wild Woods, dense with trees and foliage, the mysterious Mirage, a swirling, shimmering place, and on the farthest edge, the Glacier, a tundra of frozen ice and snow. In the center of Dragon's Claw was the Palm, the location of the Dragon Force Tower, the Great Hall, the canteen, auditorium, Arena, and training cubes.

It was a magical place, with good reason. Dragon's Claw was the headquarters of the Dragon Force— the elite group of humans and their heart-bonded dragons who worked together to protect the New World. And it was also home to Camp Claw, where potential recruits to the Dragon Force were trained and, if they were lucky, found their heart-bonded dragons. It was all because humans and dragons now needed to work together to fight against common enemies and keep their shared home safe.

When the Dragon Realm had collapsed on the Human Realm, it brought dragons and magic, as well as completely changing the world with new land masses, mountain ranges, and oceans. One of the new continents was Dracordia, mostly populated by dragons, and at the edge of Dracordia, connected by a long strip of land, was Dragon's Claw.

But dragons weren't the only new creatures coming in. When the Great Collapse happened, it tore holes in the very fabric of the universe, and suddenly there was an onslaught of attacks from new monstrous creatures of all kinds. Creatures who would attack both humans and dragons.

And so the Dragon Force was created, to protect the New World. The human and dragon members of the Dragon Force were the heroes of the New World, saving the day, time and time again.

For as long as he could remember, twelve-year-old Lance had been desperate to go to Camp Claw. All he'd wanted was to find his heart-bonded dragon and join the Dragon Force. When his flame post invitation had come, he couldn't believe it. Not only had Lance been invited, but his younger sister, Zoe, had found her heart-bonded dragon in the woods behind their house in New London. Lance had been shocked when the purple dragon had appeared to them and bonded with Zoe right then and there. Zoe was only ten, and Lance had never heard of anyone finding their dragon so young.

Then the Lo siblings had arrived at Camp Claw, and it was everything Lance could have hoped for and more. Lance had found Infinity, his dragon, and she had gifted him a magical erhu that had awakened his own power of music mastery and song spells. He'd made friends, too—Bea from Buenos Aires and Arthur from New New York. He'd thought it was the best week of his life, until suddenly everything went horribly wrong. What had started as a week of dreams coming true had quickly become a nightmare. Arthur had inadvertently been working for the Swarm, an evil genius who had been transformed into a giant beetle-man. Amid a rise of global attacks that took away the leaders of the Dragon Force from Camp Claw, the Swarm, along with creatures under his influence, attacked Camp Claw and stole the Heart Stone—the core of Dragon's Claw's magic.

Together, with their dragons, Lance and his friends had tracked down the Swarm and had taken back the Heart Stone. But when they'd returned to Camp Claw, it was deserted.

The Swarm had been a distraction. He'd been tasked with stealing the Heart Stone by the Devourer—a terrifying, all-powerful creature from a distant galaxy that was coming to the New World to devour them all. In preparation for his arrival, the Devourer had sent an ambush of Petrifiers to Dragon's Claw. Petrifiers were creatures of smoke and shadow that fought with fear, meaning they could strike so much terror into the hearts of their prey that they would be petrified—so filled with fear that they'd be unable to move. And almost all of the Dragon Force had been petrified and taken to the hidden den of the Devourer, ready for him to feast on them.

All except Lance, Zoe, Arthur, Bea, and their dragons. They had returned with the Heart Stone and put it back in its rightful place in Dragon's Claw. And they were in time to find one remaining dragon—Kronos, the Camp Claw historian, who had managed to fight the fear long enough to escape the Petrifiers and tell the group what had happened—before the fear finally broke into his heart, leaving him petrified on Dragon's Claw.

In the last moments before Kronos froze entirely,

Lance had sworn to him that they would do whatever it took to save the rest of the Dragon Force.

After they had returned the Heart Stone to where it belonged, the shell-shocked group of friends had gone to the Volcano and into their sleep pods, so they could get some rest. They needed to be at their best if they stood any chance of finding and rescuing the Dragon Force.

Lance had tried to sleep, but it felt impossible. He tossed and turned, and his body ached with exhaustion, but his mind wouldn't quiet. After what felt like hours, he had sat up and decided to go to the top of the Volcano to get some fresh air, hoping that the night breeze would soothe him.

Through his bond with Infinity, he had sensed that the dragon was awake too, and he'd asked her to meet him. Now Lance and Infinity were standing on the very top of the Volcano. The highest floor of the Volcano was the common room, in a ring around the edge, like all the other floors. But Lance had wanted to go higher than that, and so he was perching on the edge of the opening itself. It was wide enough for both him and Infinity to stand and had a small lip that curved up, so he felt confident he wouldn't fall in. From this angle he could see all the way down inside the Volcano, which still hummed and buzzed and beeped with dragon magic and technology. Even with the Dragon Force gone, the tech was still running. Neon, the giant electric-green dragon that had heart-bonded with Bea, had explained that the Volcano was infused with dragon magic, but that it didn't need dragons to run. It was almost like a living thing itself.

Lance drew strength from it—the Volcano that had already started to feel like a second home. And being able to see the stars still shining was a comfort, even as the shadow in the sky grew—which meant the Devourer was coming. The stars shone like beacons of hope. For a brief moment, everything felt as if it would be okay.

Yes, their task was enormous. And yes, they had no idea even how to begin.

But they had their dragons and one another, and Lance kept telling himself that was enough, that together they would be able to do this.

Then the breeze stopped suddenly and there was

a ringing in Lance's ears, muffling the sound of the waves on the beach below. Goose bumps rose on the back of his neck, and he felt dizzy and strange and began to sway on his feet. Every breath he took made him feel increasingly uneasy, as if he were breathing in poison.

"Infinity, do you feel that?" Lance reached for his dragon, just as the Volcano began to shake beneath them.

"Lance! Quick! On my back!" Infinity cried out as the Volcano continued to shake.

Lance leaped on his dragon's back. "Is the Volcano going to erupt?" he said. "We have to get the others!" Infinity flew up above the Volcano, and they watched it shuddering and shaking beneath them.

Infinity shook her head. "It isn't erupting—it is trying to warn us about something! It is trying to shake out an intruder!"

"Dive inside!" said Lance, and Infinity flew straight down the middle of the Volcano, wings fully back and nose down. As they raced through the central open corridor of the Volcano, Lance shouted for his sister and his friends. "Zoe! Arthur! Bea! Wake up!"

He sighed with relief when he saw his sister staggered out of her sleep pod and toward the edge of the walkway. "Zoe! Get down here!" he shouted.

Zoe leaped off the edge, her short dark-brown hair flowing out around her head like a halo. A moment later her lavender-colored dragon, Violet, zoomed in from above the Volcano, moving so quickly that she was beneath Zoe in an instant, long before Zoe had a chance of hitting the ground.

"What is it?" Zoe called out to Lance. "Is it an attack?" Violet flew close to Infinity and Lance, and Lance could see how nervous his sister was. Even though they'd been born two years apart, they had always been close, and their time at Camp Claw had brought them even closer. They even looked similar, with their dark-brown hair and dark eyes that crinkled in the corners when they smiled. The Lo siblings were dual heritage—a mix of their British Chinese father and their white British mom. Lance wanted to comfort Zoe, the way he always had, but there wasn't time for that right now.

"I don't know!" Lance admitted as he looked around the Volcano, trying to find the source of what was making it react like this. "Where are Bea and Arthur?"

"Right here!" said a voice from above him, and Lance glanced up to see Bea on the back of her bright-green dragon, Neon—they were flying down to join the group near the floor of the Volcano. Her curly brown hair was tied up in two bunches on her head, and her brown eyes were wide with worry.

"I'm here too," said another voice, and Arthur and his black-and-silver dragon, Jaws, flew down next to Lance and Infinity. "But shouldn't we be exiting the shaking Volcano instead of going deeper inside it?" Arthur, who was blond with white skin, looked even paler than usual as his eyes darted around the Volcano.

"Arthur has a point," said Bea. "We should get out of here."

"There is something in here that I do not like," said Neon in his low, almost robotic voice. "I have never seen the Volcano react like this to anything."

"Well, I came back in to make sure you guys weren't trapped inside," said Lance, still scanning their surroundings, trying to see what was making the Volcano respond this way. "But now that we are in here, all together, I think we need to figure out what is going on."

The Volcano was designed to accommodate humans and dragons—so the central corridor was wide and open, but around the edges, in a circle, sleep pods were carved into the interior walls of the Volcano, connected with long halls.

A chill filled the air, and Lance glimpsed a strange shadow darting around the circular paths that wound up around the walls of the Volcano. His eyes couldn't quite land on it, and when he tried to look at it straight on, it disappeared. Something close to fear began to spread through him.

"There," he said, pointing at it. "Something is up there, in the upper halls."

"We must stop it," said Jaws, growling low in his throat. "Before it gets out."

"How are we going to catch it?" asked Zoe. "I can't even see it!"

"Do not worry, Zoe," said Violet, tossing her head. "I can catch anything." She began to flap her wings, and a lavender-colored mist began to flow from her body. "Nothing escapes my mystifying mist." Violet was both a healer and enchanter dragon and used mist that billowed out from under her scales to either heal or harm. This signature move could confuse and entrance her victims. As she flapped her wings, the mist rose up in the air, as if it was seeking something. It moved with purpose, darting around the group of humans and dragons.

Electric sparks crackled around Neon. "I, too, am prepared to fight. We will find whatever it is that is hiding here inside our volcano, and we will destroy it," he rumbled.

"What if it is a Petrifier?" said Lance quietly. "The Petrifiers were able to petrify and capture all of the Dragon Force. What chance do we have against power like that?" As he spoke, he reached for his erhu, the stringed instrument gifted to him by Infinity. The erhu looked like a sledgehammer with two strings running from one edge of the hammer to the tip of its handle. When Lance played it, he used the bow that was interlocked between the two strings to make it sing, and he ran his fingers up and down the strings to change the notes. Lance loved how the sound echoed and reverberated in the sound box at the bottom, the part that looked like the hammer. Lance knew that the erhu was an ancient Chinese instrument, still used in modern times, and usually the bow was made of horsehair. But his bow was made of dragon hair, willingly given to create the instrument and enhance it with dragon magic. And that wasn't the only special thing about his erhu. When he played it, he could summon spells with his song. Spells for protection, for defense, for more than he could imagine. And the erhu itself could be used as a powerful, magical hammer that could break through all kinds of things. When he wasn't using it, Lance wore the erhu on his back with an unbreakable strap. Lance was glad to always have it close, just in case he needed it. His erhu, and his power that had come from his dragon-bond with Infinity, had saved the lives of he and his friends when they had battled the Swarm. The Swarm had started life as a human named Frank Albert before he'd been turned into a giant beetle-man from a magical essence known as "golden elixir." The Swarm hated dragons, and he was intent on destroying dragonkind and serving the Devourer in the hope that he would be rewarded with infinite power.

Lance knew it was inevitable that he and his friends would face the Devourer, but he hoped that by the time they did, they would have saved the Dragon Force. Together they would be strong enough to take on the creature so powerful and mighty that he could travel across the universe with ease, devouring entire worlds as he went. The very thought of the Devourer terrified Lance. It seemed impossible that the Devourer could be defeated, especially as he had sent the Petrifiers to the New World first, to find the greatest sources of power for him to feast on when he arrived, and that the Petrifiers had been able to petrify and kidnap all of the members of the Dragon Force. The Petrifiers supposedly had a mere fraction of the amount of power that the Devourer had.

And yet the Petrifiers had still been able to defeat the strongest group in the New World: the leaders of the Dragon Force and their dragons.

Lance knew he and his friends couldn't give up now, no matter how bleak it seemed. They had to try to find the rest of Dragon Force before the Devourer arrived.

"The Dragon Force were unprepared for the Petrifiers," said Jaws. "We will not be caught unawares." He snapped his teeth. "And I am ready for it—be it a Petrifier or some other creature."

A low howl echoed all around them, and Lance felt his skin prickle with unease.

"I'm scared," whispered Zoe. And Lance, too, was filled with a creeping dread. The group drew in closer together.

Infinity's four gemstones on her horns began to glow. "Block out the fear. You must not let it overcome you."

There was another howl, and the air grew colder. Lance looked up and saw the strange shadow again, but this time it was leaping right toward him.

Cold Smoke

"Look out!" Lance shouted, and Infinity moved out of the way just in time. The shadow creature landed next to them, snarling and snapping its jaws.

Now that it was closer, Lance realized it was quite wolf-like in appearance, with a long snout and pointy ears, but a long serpent-like body. It was smaller than he was expecting, about the size of a large dog, and looked like a cross between a wolf and a snake—but instead of fur it had long tendrils of shadow and smoke, making it look smudged at the edges.

But its teeth and claws were solid, made clear by the clicking of its claws on the Volcano's floor and the snapping of its jaws.

Sunk deep in its head were glowing red eyes. Eyes that were focused on Lance. He felt as if he couldn't move, as if he was trapped in its gaze. His mouth went dry.

"It is so small," rumbled Neon. "I should not be afraid of it, and yet I feel a fear in my chest like nothing I have ever experienced."

The creature bared its teeth, and wisps of shadow began to flow from it toward them, like ropes with minds of their own.

Lance tried to speak but it felt as if his jaws were fused together. Finally, he forced the words out. "Use your mist to fight it, Violet!"

"I am trying," said Violet, "but my powers feel blocked, as if they have been frozen inside me."

Lance knew then with certainty that the creature was what he had feared.

A lone Petrifier. Left on purpose or by accident, he wasn't sure. But he realized that despite knowing that they might face one, they were woefully unprepared.

How could they battle this creature if they could not move?

With increasing horror, he noticed that the tendrils of shadow flowing from the Petrifier were wrapping around his neck and even trying to wriggle into his nose and mouth. He began to cough.

"Do not let it in!" roared Jaws. "If it gets inside you, that is how you will be petrified."

"How can we stop it?" Arthur said in a strained voice. "I can barely speak, and my whole body already feels frozen! Is this the start of being petrified?"

"This is how it begins," said Neon.

"You must not be afraid!" said Infinity. "A Petrifier's power can only truly get inside you if you let fear take over."

"But I am afraid!" Zoe's voice came out in a squeak, and the Petrifier's shadows began to flow faster toward her, as if it could hear her fear. As if the shadows themselves could scent it. The shadow wolf began to howl with glee, edging closer to Zoe and Violet. Violet let out a snarl, but she still seemed frozen by the Petrifier's power.

"I cannot summon fire or mist or anything!" Violet cried out. Before this moment, Lance had not known that dragons could even feel fear. But he saw the panic in Violet's eyes as she strained to protect her heart-bonded human but wasn't able to do anything.

"Help!" Zoe's voice cracked as the Petrifier's shadowy ropes began to wrap around her like pythons.

The fear in Zoe's voice made Lance's own fear disappear. Instead, he was filled with rage. He wasn't going to let some shadow wolf petrify his little sister. No. It would have to go through him first.

Good, thought Infinity down their bond. *Right now, anger is better than fear. And loyalty and love and bravery are best of all.* She sent a surge of her own strength. *You can do this, Lance. You can break free, and then we all can.*

And suddenly Lance found that he could move again. Feeling returned to his body, and he felt the familiar rush of warmth that came with a burst of Infinity's power.

With a bellowing cry, Lance leaped off Infinity and landed directly in front of the shadow-wolf Petrifier. It yelped, and its smoke tendrils retracted. As they whipped past Lance, he flinched.

They were so cold that they burned.

Cold smoke. It felt unnatural and strange, just like this smoke and shadow creature in front of him with glowing eyes and sharp teeth.

But he would not be afraid. He slipped off his erhu and began to play the first thing that came to him. A song of strength and power, a song of bravery. The song washed over his friends and their dragons, and they, too, began to move.

Lance grinned as he played faster now, expertly moving the bow between the strings.

The Petrifier retracted its smoke wisps even farther and seemed to shrink in front of them. It bared its teeth, and Lance sensed it was confused.

For a brief moment, he felt pity for it. It was far from wherever it had come from and had been separated from the others like it.

But then it lashed out, this time toward Bea, and Lance hardened his heart against the Petrifier. They needed to learn how to defeat it if they ever wanted to rescue the Dragon Force.

"Nice try!" cried Bea, nimbly leaping out of the way and back onto Neon's back. "Thanks, Lance! Your song unfroze me!" She intertwined her fingers and cracked her knuckles. "Now, time for me to give that Petrifier something to be afraid of. Neon! Electric net!"

As Bea spoke, the Petrifier changed size again, and shape as well. It began to grow and started to look more like a bear than a wolf, roaring in anger.

The dragons roared back, and then Bea and Neon blasted it with an electric net, trapping it in buzzing green streams of pure electricity. The shadow-bear Petrifier bellowed again, but when it tried to send out another one of its smoke wisps, they sizzled when they hit the electric net.

"Not so scary anymore, are you?" said Arthur. Lance noticed that he scooted a little bit behind Jaws, his massive black-and-silver dragon, as he spoke.

The Petrifier hissed.

Then, to Lance's shock, it spoke. The voice was low and sonorous, and otherworldly.

"I smell great power here." The voice echoed all around them, and the eyes of the Petrifier changed from burning red to a glowing white, like two stars shining.

The voice made them all freeze again. It was like

nothing Lance had ever heard, and it seemed to echo in his very bones. He realized suddenly, with a fresh wave of terror, that they were hearing the voice of the Devourer himself. He wasn't sure how he knew it, but it felt instinctive, as if he were an animal faced with his greatest predator. He wanted to run, to hide, but he could not move.

"You may have trapped one of my Petrifiers, but that was just one of millions. I create them. They are formed from the very hairs on my back, and they soar through the universe and do my bidding. Seeking out the magic I hunger for. And here..."

The shadow-bear Petrifier stopped speaking and lifted its snout in the air, sniffing loudly. "Here is the most delicious power." The Petrifier turned its gaze back on them, and its white eyes were so bright and so piercing it was like staring directly into the midday sun. But Lance couldn't look away, couldn't close his eyes, couldn't do anything but stand there. "I will consume you all."

The shadow-bear Petrifier howled again, but this time Lance knew they were hearing the howl of the Devourer. And then the white eyes of the Petrifier glowed even more brightly, the two eyes merging into one, and the creature shrank and shrank, disappearing into the one white eye, until all that was left was one glowing white orb floating in the buzzing electric net.

Lance sensed it a moment before it happened.

"WATCH OUT!" he cried, just as what was left of the Petrifier exploded.

An Impossible Task

The force of the Petrifier's explosion flung Lance and the others back against the wall of the Volcano. Even the dragons could not withstand it, and the sound of their powerful bodies smacking against the Volcano wall was one of the worst things Lance had ever heard.

But the dragons had all somehow been able to protect their humans, twisting their bodies for their humans to land on, instead of on the Volcano's stony interior.

Lance knew with a sickening certainty that if any of them had hit the wall, they would have broken their necks. As it was, Lance felt as if he had been in a car crash. But he knew it could have been so much worse. Their dragons had protected them.

Infinity, did I hurt you? He had landed against her

back, and her wings were splayed at a strange angle against the Volcano's wall.

Of course not. I might be small for a dragon, but I am still a dragon.

Just making sure.

"Is everyone okay?" Lance said out loud. His voice came out in a croak. "Zoe? Arthur? Bea?"

Arthur cracked open one eye. "Define 'okay.'"

"I'll take that as a yes," said Lance. He forced himself to stand and stumbled to where Zoe and Violet lay in a heap. "Zoe?" What if his sister was hurt? What if she didn't respond? All the worst-case scenarios flashed through his mind.

Zoe slowly lifted her head, and Lance was flooded with relief.

"I'm okay," she said.

"Me too," said Bea, adjusting her glasses.

Neon let out a groan. "That was deeply unpleasant."

Violet snorted. "It was the worst thing I have ever experienced, and I once battled a giant six-headed goat in Dracordia."

"Are we sure it is gone?" Lance looked over at the space where the Petrifier had been, and all that was left was a scorch mark on the Volcano's floor. "Why did it explode like that?"

"The Volcano has calmed," said Jaws. "That is a good sign."

It was true—the Volcano was no longer shaking.

"If the Petrifier remained inside, the Volcano would still be trying to expel it," Jaws went on.

"But where did it go?" said Bea, tilting her head back and looking at the opening of the Volcano. "And is it alive?"

"The Petrifiers are an extension of the Devourer," said Neon. "It was never alive. Imagine if I could remove my claws and send them into another galaxy, and somehow still control them, and even feel what they were feeling. The claws would not be alive, nor would they be dead. But I think that particular Petrifier is no longer anywhere near us."

"At least now we know more about what we are up against," said Lance. "And that they can be contained. And just one wasn't able to petrify us."

"That is why the Devourer made it explode," said Infinity. "Because he knew we were learning about it. And that makes us more powerful."

"But the Devourer now knows more about us too," Arthur pointed out. "Didn't you all hear that extremely creepy thing he said about our smell?"

"I already knew I smelled wonderful," said Violet, with a toss of her head.

Bea burst out laughing. "I don't think that is what he meant, Violet." Zoe giggled a little, and even Arthur cracked a smile.

Lance wanted to laugh too—wanted to celebrate that they were still alive, that the Petrifier hadn't managed to fully petrify them—but he still felt too tense, as if the Petrifier could appear again at any moment. What if there were more?

"Do you think the Devourer left that one behind on purpose?" he asked, looking to the dragons for their opinion. "Or was it an accident?"

"It is impossible to know," replied Jaws.

Zoe tugged on the ends of her hair, and Lance knew she only did that when she was anxious. "Will the Devourer send more Petrifiers after us?" she asked. "To, you know, finish the job."

"Most likely," said Jaws. "But I do not know how long it will take for them to arrive. The Devourer himself moves slowly through the universe, so we hopefully have enough time to prepare."

Arthur let out a long sigh. "It feels as if we don't even have a chance. This is impossible. We'll never be able to defeat the Devourer."

"We have to try," said Lance. "We can't give up before we start."

"Lance, didn't you feel the power radiating off that creature? That is *one* hair of the Devourer, literally, and it made us all so afraid, we were almost totally petrified."

"But we were able to stop it," Lance pointed out.

"Barely." Arthur crossed his arms.

Annoyance bubbled up inside Lance. "Why are you being so negative?" He wanted them all to be on the same side, to be hopeful. And Arthur was giving up before they had even started.

"I'm being rational," Arthur snapped back.

"Arguing isn't going to help anyone," said Bea. "I think we are all a little bit in shock. It has been an intense few days—and it is the middle of the night."

"Bea is right. You all are exhausted," added Neon. "You need rest."

"We can't rest!" Lance blurted out. "We are running out of time! The Devourer now knows about us!"

"And what if there are more Petrifiers hiding on Dragon's Claw and they come out while we are sleeping?" said Zoe. "I agree with Lance." But as she spoke, Lance could see she was wobbly on her feet, and he felt a pang of guilt when he realized how exhausted his sister was.

"*We* will not sleep. *You* will sleep. Dragons don't need the same amount of sleep as humans, remember? And we will make sure that nothing harms you while you get your rest." Violet gently nudged Zoe with her head, and Lance knew the dragon was trying to comfort his sister. "I can use my healing power to make sure that the sleep is the best you have ever had, and you will all wake up refreshed after only a few hours."

Lance wasn't convinced. "I still think we should try to find the other Petrifiers right now."

"Lance, you cannot battle the Devourer if you are burned out and exhausted," said Infinity. "You still need to recover from the battle with the Swarm. I can sense how tired your body is."

Lance scowled at his dragon, feeling slightly betrayed that Infinity had told the others about his exhaustion.

"Battling the Devourer is like the tenth step of what we need to do," said Bea, her eyebrows furrowing over the top of her glasses as she listed things off on her fingers. "First we need to figure out where the Petrifiers took the Dragon Force, then how we get there, then we'll need to think about how we'll battle a whole army of Petrifiers and keep ourselves from being petrified, and what our plan is to unpetrify the Dragon Force . . ." Her voice trailed off. "The dragons are right. We definitely need to get some sleep before we attempt all of that."

"See, this is my whole point," said Arthur. "This is too much for us to take on! We will never be able to do this. No matter how much sleep we get!"

"Not with that attitude," said Lance, frowning at his friend.

"I just don't believe we are the heroes you think we are!"

"Why did you come to Camp Claw at all if you don't want to be a hero?" said Zoe, putting her hands on her hips. "Isn't the whole point that you train up, and if you are good enough, you are invited to join the Dragon Force and help to protect the New World?"

"Exactly! And we aren't good enough! We've been here for less than a week! We aren't the Dragon Force. We are *kids*. We can't protect anyone! We need protecting!" Arthur sounded close to tears as he glared at all of them. "And the reason I came to Camp Claw was to seek revenge on dragons, remember?" The Swarm had tricked Arthur into thinking that dragons had killed his father, when it had been the Swarm all along. He had then manipulated Arthur into helping him attack Camp Claw. Lance knew Arthur was still racked with guilt about it.

"But then you found Jaws! And us! And you realized you were wrong about dragons," said Bea.

Arthur let out a long breath and ran his hand through his hair. "I just think I want to go home."

Lance stared at him, suddenly filled with rage. "Nobody will stop you. I'm sure Jaws could fly you home." He couldn't believe what he was hearing. Give up? Go home? Leave them at an even bigger disadvantage? "But if the Devourer comes, and he succeeds, you won't have a home to go back to."

Arthur paled and swallowed audibly. Lance's anger dissipated, and he felt a little mean for being so blunt. But he had to make Arthur understand. "We need you, Arthur," he added after a moment. He didn't want to force Arthur to be there, but he wanted him to know that he was needed. He was part of their team.

"Lance is right," rumbled Jaws. "Arthur, I can see inside your heart, and I know you are brave. You can do this."

Arthur scrunched up his face tight, as if he was trying not to cry. "I feel as if this is all my fault. If I hadn't trusted the Swarm, if I hadn't let him in . . ."

"There is no point in trying to change what has already happened," Neon interrupted. "You made a mistake. All humans make mistakes."

"And we all forgave you," rumbled Jaws, stepping closer to Arthur. Jaws gazed around at the rest of the group. "Right?"

"Of course," said Lance.

Zoe nodded. "Definitely. As Neon said, everyone makes mistakes."

"What about dragons?" said Bea. "Do they ever make mistakes?"

"Very rarely," said Violet with a sniff. Then she flew toward Arthur. "Do not make trusting you one of our mistakes."

"Back away from my human," growled Jaws.

"Tell your human to stop whining," Violet snapped back. "And to show a little more strength of spirit."

"I don't want to be the weak link," said Arthur.

"You aren't the weak link," said Lance. "We need you. We're stronger together, remember?" He went over to his friend and put a hand on his shoulder. "We believe in you, Arthur. Now you need to believe in yourself."

"I don't want to die. Or get petrified," Arthur said quietly.

Lance let out a laugh. "Bro, me neither! We are going to do everything we can to make sure that *doesn't* happen." He gave Arthur an encouraging grin. "So, are you in?"

Arthur closed his eyes for a moment, taking a deep breath, and then when he opened them, he smiled back.

"Yes!" said Lance, fist-pumping the air.

"That's more like it," said Bea, with a wide smile.

"Okay, now that we are all back on the same side," said Zoe. "What next?"

"Now you sleep," said Infinity. "Remember? That is what started this whole argument!"

Lance yawned, letting himself feel how exhausted he really was. "You know what? I am too tired to insist that I'm not tired."

Zoe, Arthur, and Bea laughed.

"Me too," said Zoe.

"So it is settled, then. The humans sleep and recover, we stand guard, and then tomorrow we track down the Petrifiers," said Jaws.

"I think we should all stay together, though, while we sleep," said Lance. "Just in case."

"Good idea," said Bea. "But this is the only spot that can fit all the dragons."

"Then this is where we're sleeping," said Lance. Then he turned to his dragon. "Infinity, can you close the top of the Volcano? I mean properly seal it shut so nothing can get in?" Infinity had an affinity with the Volcano, and Lance had seen her open holes in the side of it, so he guessed she could close it too.

"I have never tried, but I think so," said Infinity. "Hold on." She flew to the top of the Volcano, and Lance watched in awe as the four gemstones on her head began to glow. Slowly the top of the Volcano began to close, as if it were made of clay and being molded by invisible hands.

"While Infinity seals the Volcano, Violet and I can go and get everyone's pillows and blankets," said Zoe. "If we are sleeping on the floor here, I want to be comfy!"

Bea laughed. "Good idea, Zoe."

"I am not a blanket-delivery dragon," grumbled Violet, but she flew with Zoe to the sleep pods anyway.

Once they had turned the floor of the Volcano into a more comfortable sleeping place, Lance finally felt his adrenaline from the past two days fade, and exhaustion took over.

He lay down, and Infinity settled next to him. Lance felt comforted by her nearness. His erhu was under his pillow, and that, too, was a comfort. The others found their spots, the children in the center of a circle of dragons, with each dragon closest to their heart-bonded human. Violet began to hum and flap her wings, and a sweet-scented mist floated out from her scales, drifting over them.

"This will help you sleep," Violet said, her tone gentler than Lance had ever heard it. "And it will heal any aches or pains you have from today."

Lance took a deep breath and immediately felt more relaxed and at peace. The last thought he had before sleep claimed him was that if the Devourer really was coming, at least he and his sister had found their dragons before the world ended.

The Hunt for Hints

Lance woke up with a jolt.

He was sleeping, his head on Infinity's side, next to his friends. All of them were sprawled out across the Volcano floor.

The memory of the evening before came flooding back. The Petrifier. The argument with Arthur.

He had no idea what time it was now. How long they had been sleeping. He scrambled to his feet, adrenaline coursing through him. Surely they had slept too long? He felt so well-rested, as if he had been sleeping for days.

"Infinity, how long have we been sleeping?" His voice came out in a croak. Infinity blinked at him.

"Time means different things to dragons," she said.

Lance sighed and ran his hand across his face. "You know what I mean! In . . . human time! In hours!"

"Dragons are not alarm clocks," said Violet from across the Volcano floor. Her voice was haughty. "But it has only been a few hours. We know, even more than you, how much is at stake. How we cannot waste any time. But, before you berate us for time passing, I would like to say you are very welcome for helping you and your friends sleep so well. Do you not feel fully healed and exceptionally well-rested?"

Lance bowed his head, feeling chastened. "Sorry," he said. "I'm just anxious about . . . well, everything. But you're right." He glanced up and grinned at Violet. "Your healing powers are amazing. I feel great."

Violet tossed her head. "I do not need a human to tell me that I am good at what I do." She sniffed. "But I would appreciate a thank-you."

"Thank you," Lance said, and he meant it.

The others were beginning to wake. Zoe stretched and rubbed her eyes, and Lance saw the same confusion and panic that he had just experienced flash across her face. He hurried over to his sister.

"Everything is fine," he said. "Or at least as fine as it was when we went to sleep." Then he grinned at Violet again. "Actually, it is better now, because your awesome dragon put us into a super-sleep and healed us all."

"You do not need to go on and on." Violet sounded almost embarrassed. "You said thank you as I requested, and now you have made your point."

Lance laughed.

Bea yawned as she sat up. "Did anything happen in the night?"

"If anything happened outside the Volcano, we have not detected it," rumbled Neon. "What was left of the Petrifier has not returned, and we believe it has gone for good."

"And we know that nothing else entered the Volcano," added Jaws. "The roof was sealed, and we have been on alert."

"Thanks, Jaws," said Arthur, standing to pat his dragon on the side. "So what now?"

Lance felt the weight of what had happened to the Dragon Force settle on his shoulders again, like a heavy coat he had taken off while he'd slept and now had to put back on. Arthur, Bea, and Zoe all looked at him expectantly. As if he should know what to do next. Somehow, between them all meeting and the battle with the Swarm and the return to Dragon's Claw, he had become the one they looked to as leader. And he couldn't let them down. He took a deep breath.

"Now we try to find a clue for where the Petrifiers took the Dragon Force. And ... we go from there. At least now we know that it is possible to defeat a Petrifier."

"Possible to defeat *one* Petrifier that was left behind. Probably because it was the weakest of the bunch," said Arthur. "I suspect it is actually impossible to defeat more than one."

"Arthur, we're going to be positive, remember?" said Bea, elbowing him in the ribs.

Arthur scowled at her, but Bea just grinned back at him. "Turn that frown upside down! Time to find some clues!"

"Are you always this cheerful?" Arthur grumbled.

"My mama said I was born smiling," Bea replied with a smirk. "So, yes."

"All right, all right. I'll be cheerful!" Arthur gave them all an exaggerated smile. "How is this?"

"Terrifying, but an improvement," said Bea.

"Is that what I look like when I smile?" Infinity murmured, baring all of her teeth in demonstration.

Arthur rolled his eyes as everyone else laughed.

"Where do we start looking for clues?" asked Zoe.

This time Lance looked to Infinity. She knew Dragon's Claw better than anyone.

"I think we should go back to where we found Kronos," Infinity said softly. "He was the only one here who saw the actual attack. And even if he cannot speak or move, there may be a hint near him."

It felt strange, flying through an empty Camp Claw. Lance was so used to it buzzing, with recruits and dragons everywhere. He scanned the ground below, looking for something, anything, to give them a clue about where the Petrifiers had gone.

At least the land itself was alive and thriving. After Lance and the others had returned the Heart Stone back to its rightful place, the land had turned back from stone to earth, the grass becoming a vibrant green, and magic flowed freely through Dragon's Claw once more.

Lance only wished that the magic had been enough to unpetrify Kronos.

Kronos, the ancient dragon who was Camp Claw's historian, keeper of the history of dragons, had been taken by the Petrifiers but had managed to escape their net and fall back down to Dragon's Claw.

But by the time that Lance had found him, fear had already taken root in the periwinkle-blue dragon, and as much as he'd fought it, he couldn't stop himself being petrified. In the moments he'd had left before he fully turned to stone, Kronos told Lance and the others what had happened. And then he stopped moving and speaking completely, his long body frozen with fear. Petrified. Even his whiskers, almost as long as his body, had hardened to stone.

Part of Lance hoped that Kronos would be gone, that he had somehow become unpetrified in the night and flown away.

But as they landed behind the canteen, where they had found him before, he was still there. Still petrified. Eyes still wide with fear, mouth open but not breathing. Lance felt an unexpected lump in his throat. It wasn't natural to see such a magnificent creature looking like this. To see a dragon frozen as still as a statue. And it was a reminder of the fate of all of the Dragon Force. For a moment, Lance thought he saw one of Kronos's eyes twitch, but it must have been a shadow, a trick of the light.

"Can he hear us?" he murmured to Infinity.

"I do not know," Infinity replied, gazing at the stone dragon. "But it does not hurt to give him some comfort."

His heart in his throat, Lance slid off Infinity and approached the petrified Kronos. He put his hand on the dragon's back. "Kronos, if you can hear me, we just wanted to let you know that we are going to find the rest of the Dragon Force. And we're going to figure out a way to unpetrify you and everyone else. Everything is going to be okay."

Neon, Violet, and Jaws all landed, with their riders on their backs. Lance felt slightly self-conscious for speaking to a stone dragon, but then Bea, Arthur, and Zoe all joined his side.

"We'll fix this, Kronos," whispered Zoe. Her voice shook, and Lance knew his sister was trying to be brave. "I promise."

"Friend," rumbled Jaws, "if you can hear us and there is a way, give us a sign for where we go next? The only thing we know is that the Dragon Force disappeared in the sky. But the sky is vast."

"Vaster than ever before," said Neon, glancing upward. "Things can come in, and things can leave."

Bea cocked her head to the side. "Is there a chance that the Petrifiers have already taken them . . ." Her voice trailed off, and she gulped.

"Through the tear in the sky to another universe?" Zoe chimed in.

"That would take an incredible amount of power— even more than the Petrifiers have. To be able to transport that many humans and their dragons, even in petrified form." Jaws shook his mighty head. "No. I suspect they are hidden, somewhere not too far, waiting for the Devourer to arrive."

"And if the Devourer feasts on them, then he will be strong enough to swallow our entire world," said Neon. "We cannot let that happen."

"This is why we have to find a clue!" said Lance, clenching his fists with determination.

"Should we call the rest of the Dragon Force, the ones still out in the field, to come and help?" said Arthur. "Surely they would be better prepared than us!"

"We cannot leave all of the New World entirely unprotected," said Jaws. "Every member of the Dragon Force who are based in the New World are there for a reason."

"You children are the only ones who have the dragons, and the power, and who are not committed to protecting an area already. If we call on all of the wider Dragon Force to come to us, there is nobody to protect the humans and dragons from anything else that falls from the sky," Neon explained.

"Or that climbs out of the oceans," added Bea, with a glance toward the sea from where the lava monsters they had previously battled had come.

"Exactly. And more important," Neon went on, turning to look at Infinity, "we have the Infinite Dragon. Infinity, I know you have lived much of your young life in hiding, but now your ability to create golden elixir has been awakened. With your heart-bonded human by your side, your powers will be greater than ever." Neon looked at the group. "Together we can find where the Petrifiers have taken the Dragon Force and unpetrify everyone, and then we will truly be unstoppable. Even the Devourer will be no match for our combined greatness."

Lance glanced at Infinity, who had gone very still. "I cannot be the key," she whispered. "I still do not know how to control my power."

Lance felt a rush of protectiveness and moved closer to his dragon. "You don't have to do it alone. I'm here now, like Neon said. We're all here, with you."

Infinity nodded. "I will do whatever I can to protect the world. To stop the Devourer. I promise that."

As she said the word "promise," her heart glowed gold, and Lance remembered something he had heard once. That a promise from a dragon could not be broken.

As they had suspected, Kronos did not speak. He stayed as still and silent as the statue he had become. After an apology for the indignity of what he was about to do, Neon thoroughly inspected Kronos, searching to see if there were any marks or hints on the stone dragon that might give them an idea of where the Petrifiers had gone.

"We are lucky he was able to tell us what he did," said Jaws. "At least now we know what did happen, even if we do not know exactly where they went."

"We need to keep searching Dragon's Claw for clues," said Lance decisively. "Should we split up to cover more ground or stay together?"

"Stay together," Zoe said immediately. "The dragons always say how much stronger, and safer, we are as a group."

"And just in case anything else unexpected shows up, we'll want to be together," added Bea. The dragons nodded their agreement.

They searched all day, desperately trying to find something, anything, that would help them on their quest to find the missing members of the Dragon Force. But other than the petrified Kronos, and the missing Dragon Force, there was no sign that the Petrifiers had ever been there. Even the grass that had dried up when the Heart Stone had been taken was vibrant and green again.

Lance felt overwhelmed and frustrated. They were running out of time, and they weren't any closer to finding the Dragon Force. Every time Lance looked up at the sky, it was still a strange green hue—and the shadow that looked like a bruise on the sky itself was still there, growing larger and more ominous.

Then, just as the sun was starting to set and Lance didn't feel as if they were any closer to figuring out where to start their search for the Petrifiers and the missing members of the Dragon Force, something occurred to him.

"Will the Dragon Force Tower be able to track them? The Dragon Force tech is so advanced, there has to be some sort of way to see where they've gone!"

"A brilliant idea," said Neon. "One I should have thought of myself. After all, technology is my speciality." He lowered his large head. "I feel foolish."

"Don't worry, Neon," said Bea, petting his head between his large horns. "Even dragons forget things sometimes."

"Rarely," sniffed Violet. "But I will admit it is a good suggestion from Lance."

"An excellent suggestion," said Jaws.

"My human has many excellent suggestions." The pride in Infinity's voice was obvious, and it made Lance beam.

"Well, come on!" he said, energized by the positive response from the dragons. "We have to go to the top of the Dragon Force Tower!"

The Falling Star

From the top of the Dragon Force Tower, Lance could see almost all of Dragon's Claw. The top floor functioned as a viewing tower, almost like the control room of a spaceship, with glass windows all around and a high-tech control pad along the edge.

"We are lucky we found and returned the Heart Stone," said Jaws, Arthur's dragon. "Without it, the magic that powers the Dragon Force Tower would have slowly drained away."

That gave Lance hope. At least they had done something right. But now, with almost all of the Dragon Force captured by the Petrifiers and no idea where they had been taken or how they would find them, the task ahead felt overwhelming and insurmountable. They had to find and rescue Billy Chan and the rest of the team before the Devourer arrived in the New World.

Lance glanced up. It was early evening, and the sky was darkening. It still had a strange green hue to it, and the shadow was getting bigger by the moment.

"Any luck tracking the team?" said Bea anxiously, peering round Neon to gaze at the whirring and beeping control screens.

Neon shook his great head slowly. "Look here. We can see when they were taken. All these blinking dots are the Dragon Force members and other Camp Claw recruits. Their suits have tracking and communication devices built into them."

Lance felt a lump in his throat, imagining how terrified the new recruits must have been when the Petrifiers arrived.

"They were here." Neon traced a line with his claw. "And then they were taken high above Dragon's Claw, so high that the Dragon Force tech stopped working, and then they disappeared."

"As if the sky itself swallowed them," said Violet solemnly.

Lance looked out into the darkening night again, feeling desperate. He reached for his erhu and did what he always did at home when he felt lost or frustrated or alone—he began to play. The feel of the bow in his hands and the song from the strings always calmed him and helped clear his mind.

The sound that came now was one of desperation, a cry for help. The notes built and crescendoed into a plea that sounded into the night. A plea for something, anything, that would guide them.

And then an answer came.

It was quiet at first, starting as a hum and then growing into a song of its own.

Lance recognized it. He put down his erhu and let the answering song echo all around them.

"Do you hear that?" Lance couldn't quite believe it had worked. A star had sung back to him. It felt incredible and impossible.

Infinity nodded. "I do."

"So do I," said Zoe, beaming with excitement.

"Me too," added Arthur in an incredulous tone.

"It is the singing of a star," said Infinity. "But I cannot tell what it is saying."

"Look!" said Lance, pointing out of the window.

Streaming down through the sky was a falling star, and as it came closer, its song grew louder. The group watched in awe as the star plummeted into the inky waters of the Deep Dark, leaving a shimmering trail for a moment, before disappearing completely.

"We have to find that star," said Lance. "Come on!"

The group flew out of the top of the Dragon Force Tower and toward the Deep Dark lagoon. They landed on the edge of the cliff that fell away to the Deep Dark and peered in. It was the closest Lance had been to the lagoon, as it was off limits to new recruits. But now there were no rules to follow, no leaders to listen to. As Lance gazed into the Deep Dark, he realized how unsettling it was. It appeared thick and viscous, more like ink than water. It looked like a pool of shadow you'd never emerge from if you fell in. He tried to see if he could spot any of the huge creatures that they had learned about during Camp Claw, but all he saw was darkness. Whatever lurked beneath remained unseen, like a wolf in hiding.

"None of us are trained to go into the Deep Dark," said Neon, breaking the silence. "I myself have never been in it."

"Nor I," added Jaws.

"I certainly have not," said Violet.

"Infinity?" Lance asked. Infinity was connected to Dragon's Claw in a way that none of the other dragons were: she knew its secrets and felt at home here.

Infinity paused. "I have only been in the Deep Dark once, and I found it so frightening that I haven't been back since."

Lance gulped. If Infinity found the Deep Dark scary, there was no doubt it really was terrifying. But he'd heard the song of the shooting star, and it was calling to them. Lance knew in his heart the star was trying to tell them something about what had happened to the Dragon Force. After all, the stars saw everything.

"Dragons," he said, addressing all of them. "Can any of you do an enchantment so the four of us"—he gestured to himself, Zoe, Bea and Arthur—"will be able to breathe underwater?"

"Of course," said Violet. "Such an enchantment would be easy for me."

"What about being able to see?" said Zoe, and Lance remembered that despite her bravery, his sister had always been a little afraid of the dark.

"It is called the Deep Dark for a reason," said Jaws. "Even the Dragon Force do not know how deep it is, and the darkness is absolute. The water that fills the lagoon has magical properties that smothers light itself."

"So how are we meant to find the shooting star?" said Arthur, his voice higher than usual. "I don't want to swim in darkness forever, even if we can breathe down there!"

"Maybe your pathfinding power can help us!" said Bea, her eyes lighting up. All four of them had powers that had been awakened when they had found their heart-bonded dragons. Arthur's pathfinding power was still being developed—he could find his way almost anywhere and could sense where he was in relation to his surroundings, and even track items. Bea had an affinity for molecule magic, a power that many dragons used as well, and that any dragon-bonded human could train in, but her skills were heightened. She could rearrange actual molecules in items to create new things and was especially gifted with electronics. And Zoe . . . well, Lance still couldn't quite believe his little sister's power. Zoe could replicate herself—and they weren't just projections or holograms. Zoe's replicas had real physical forms. They were like puppet extensions of herself, but even though she controlled them, she didn't feel pain if they were struck down. Lance wondered how far the replicas could exist outside Zoe, how much she could control them.

"Good thinking," he said now to Bea, turning to Arthur. "Do you think you could try?"

Arthur nodded. He turned toward the Deep Dark and closed his eyes, touching his fingertips to his temples. The children and their dragons watched as he focused, his nose scrunching up and his fingers trembling slightly. A few moments later, he opened his eyes. "Ugh," he let out, turning back to the group. "I can't get through the darkness. I hold a map of the entire New World in my mind, but when I try to see what is in this lagoon, the part of the map I'm looking for is missing." He frowned. "I'm sorry, guys. I guess my power isn't as useful as we all thought. If I can't even find my way through the Deep Dark, how am I going to help us find the Petrifiers?"

"The Deep Dark is made to be impenetrable," said Jaws. "I would have been shocked if you had been able to see in it."

"So how do we get to the star?" said Zoe, looking into the dark liquid.

"Zoe," said Lance, the idea coming on quickly. "Do you think you could replicate yourself and send your replica into the Deep Dark?"

Zoe shrugged. "I can try!" She closed her eyes and put her hand on her chest. Suddenly another Zoe popped into existence, landing in a crouch at the real Zoe's feet.

"This is so weird," murmured Bea.

"I heard that," said Zoe, opening her eyes, and grinning at her replica. "Okay, you go in the Deep Dark, and . . ." Zoe's grin faded. "Lance, what do you want the replica to do?"

"Find the star?" Lance gave her a lopsided smile. "Or . . . just test the waters to make sure that a monstrous creature isn't waiting to swallow us whole."

"You want me to use my replica as bait?" exclaimed Zoe.

"No! Not exactly. Just . . . maybe it can see what is in there and you can let us know what it sees?"

Zoe scowled at her brother, and as she did, Violet bared her teeth at him. Even the replica glared at him. "It isn't like a robot version of myself, Lance!"

"Have we figured out what exactly it is, anyway?" Arthur poked the arm of the Zoe replica and in an instant, it cartwheeled away from him.

"Your replicas definitely have better gymnastics skills than you do," Lance pointed out. "No offense."

"I don't know exactly how it works!" Zoe burst out. "Do any of you know how your powers work? No! I didn't think so! And I am trying to master mine!"

Lance went over to his sister. "I'm sorry, Zoe. I shouldn't have asked you to make your replica go into the Deep Dark."

"I'm not scared," said Zoe quickly, and a moment later her replica dived into the Deep Dark. But as it hit the surface, it evaporated.

"Oh!" said Zoe, mouth open in surprise. "I wasn't expecting that."

"As I told you," said Jaws, "the Deep Dark is impenetrable. We cannot trick it."

"Will that happen to us if we go in it?" said Bea, anxiously shifting her weight from foot to foot. "What if it doesn't like us and evaporates us?"

"Humans have been in before," said Neon. "Rarely, but it has happened. Lola often went in."

Lola Lam was one of the senior members of the Dragon Force, and her heart-bonded dragon was Neptune, a giant sea dragon, and the largest dragon Lance had ever seen. Thinking about Lola, and the rest of the Dragon Force, gave him a sharp pang in his chest. He wished that they were here to guide them—they would know what to do.

And then he remembered the reason they weren't here, and that they would never be back if he and his friends didn't figure out how to save them.

And a singing star had just fallen from the same sky into which the Dragon Force had disappeared.

"Can I use my erhu down there?" he said. "I know that Arthur's and Zoe's powers didn't work, but what about the erhu? Do you think if I play it, it might help guide me through the dark to the star? And hopefully keep whatever monsters that are in there away from us?"

"It is worth trying," said Neon thoughtfully.

"I agree," said Infinity. "Lance and I can lead the way. We can hear the song the best and we will follow it to the star. Even in the dark, even in the water, we will hear the star's song." Lance could feel that Infinity sounded more confident than she felt. He knew she was right—that their affinity to music and to the stars meant that they would be able to hear it more clearly than the others.

"Just like whales who can hear each other singing in the sea," said Bea.

"What about the rest of us?" asked Arthur. "How are we supposed to communicate down there if we can't see each other or speak? We don't all have magic instruments to play. And don't tell me I'm being negative! I'm being practical. If we all go in there, well, we'll just lose one another. What are we going to do? Hold hands?"

There was a moment of silence as the rest of the group considered Arthur's point.

Bea cleared her throat. "I don't usually agree with Arthur," she started.

Arthur scoffed.

Bea rolled her eyes and kept talking. "But he does have a point."

Lance clenched his fists to steady them. He knew he needed to take charge, even if he was afraid. "Infinity and I will go alone. The two of us will be able to communicate with each other. And she has the most experience in the Deep Dark. It doesn't make sense for all of us to go. We won't be able to see or help one another and it will just put more of us in danger." Lance could see his sister was about to protest, but he spoke over her. "Besides, some of us should stay here and keep watch in case any Petrifiers come back."

"You are the one who said we should stick together!" Zoe said. "I don't want you to disappear into there!"

"Zoe, I won't disappear. I'll be with Infinity. She knows the Deep Dark better than any of the other dragons. I'll be okay. I promise."

Zoe wiped her nose on the sleeve of her super-suit. "You don't know that." Her voice was wobbling, and Lance knew she was fighting back tears.

"I have to believe it," said Lance. "Otherwise, I'll never go in and we'll never know what that star is trying to tell us."

"Your brother is right," said Violet, swishing her tail. "And now that it has been decided he is the one to go, I can perform the enchantment so he can breathe down there." Her eyes flashed a brilliant white, and tendrils of electric-purple smoke swirled from her nostrils. She turned to Lance. "In a moment, you will lose your ability to breathe air. Do not panic, because it means you can breathe in the Deep Dark. I will give you the gills you need, and when you resurface, they will vanish and you will breathe air again."

Bea scrunched her nose. "Growing gills sounds... unpleasant."

"I said the enchantment would be easy for me—I did not say it would be pleasant for you humans." Her eyes shone at Lance. "Are you ready?"

Lance swallowed the lump that had formed in his throat and nodded.

Violet's eyes flashed as she swiftly lifted one of her claws and made three short incisions on each side of his neck. It stung, but only for a moment. Lance tried to take a breath but no air would come.

"Go now. You will be able to breathe in the water once your gills are fully formed."

Lance leaped onto Infinity's back, and without waiting another moment, his dragon dived into the Deep Dark.

The Deep Dark

The Deep Dark was much colder than Lance had expected. He had thought his super-suit would protect him from the cold, but it felt as if the liquid darkness was seeping into the suit, and further than that—into his bones. His chest tightened. He couldn't see. He couldn't breathe. He felt as if the lagoon was smothering him, swallowing him whole. He couldn't tell which way was up or down, and panic began to swirl inside him.

Lance. You need to relax. Breathe. You're okay! You have gills now. Breathe!

Lance felt a warmth in his chest as Infinity spoke to him through their bond. And then he felt . . . not exactly air, but he no longer had the urge to breathe. His gills were working!

Don't worry, Lance. Together we can do anything. Focus on finding the star.

Lance tried to focus, but the darkness was overwhelming. And then he heard the music. All his senses seemed to blur together, but the sound—there it was. It was the sound of the star.

Infinity heard it too. *We must follow the song. Let it be our guide.*

The two of them went deeper and deeper into the liquid darkness. Lance held on to Infinity's neck, their bond holding them effortlessly together as they dived into the Deep Dark. The water grew colder and thicker the deeper they went. And although they couldn't see, Lance knew that they weren't alone in the Deep Dark. As they descended, he could sense sharp movements flickering around them like blades in the water.

Still, they went farther. Lance began to lose track of time, and all he could focus on was the cold of the water, the feeling of Infinity beneath him, and the still-distant sound of the star. Lance wondered if they would get lost down here, if he would swim in this darkness until he died. And then, after Lance felt as if they had gone so deep they might be near the center of the planet, he saw a faint, sparkling light. He blinked in the dark, the light completely unexpected and beautiful after swimming so long with nothing.

I see the star!

But the music is coming from another direction, Infinity thought back.

No. It had to be the star. Lance was sure of it. What else would flicker like that, drawing him toward it? *I thought starlight could shine in the Deep Dark*, he replied. *What other light can it be?*

Lance pushed Infinity toward the light, using their bond to take control of their flight. It was one of the things Lance loved the most about his dragon-bond; they could fly as one. Through their bond they were copilots, able to control each other's movements. It took a tremendous amount of trust, and his instructors at Camp Claw had said it was rare to have such a strong dragon-bond. Lance was grateful to have such a special connection with Infinity.

Lance, wait! But Lance pushed on. He felt drawn to the light in a way that meant it had to be the star.

As they approached the light, it swung away from them, and in the faint glow, Lance realized with dawning horror that it wasn't a star but a light at the end of an enormous creature's tail.

The beast looked almost like a dragon, if a dragon had the head of a giant shark and what looked like a razor-sharp rhino horn protruding from the middle of its forehead. It had a huge, distended stomach and an incredibly long tail, with a flickering light on the end. The beast had lifted its tail so it was dangling over its own body with the light just in front of its mouth, and in the glow Lance saw that the creature was translucent. He could see all its teeth—hundreds and hundreds of them inside its massive head—and he could even see the organs inside its body.

As Lance gaped at it, trying to process what he was seeing, he suddenly remembered a fish he had learned about in school—an angler fish that lived in the deep sea and used light to draw in its victims.

Just like this sea-beast had done to him and Infinity.

Unless there was a possibility that this creature was a friend?

All of these thoughts flew through Lance's mind in a second, and by the time he realized that they should be swimming away from the giant hundred-toothed sea monster, the beast had begun to whip its tail around them at high speed, creating a whirlpool that was drawing them closer to it. This was not a friend.

Infinity, swim! They had to get away from this creature. Lance tried to keep himself from panicking, but he was terrified.

I am not as strong in water, especially not the waters of the Deep Dark, Infinity thought back, frantically straining against the force of the whirlpool. Lance could feel her panic, and this scared him most of all.

What is this thing? And why can it glow in the Deep Dark? I thought only stars could!

A shark-dragon. I have never encountered one. They are hatched in the Deep Dark and must have evolved to have light that can glow even here.

If it is a dragon, maybe we can try to reason with it! Lance was leaning back now, instinctively trying to get away from the shark-dragon as it drew them closer.

This beast is not a dragon. A shark-dragon has some dragon elements, but not a dragon heart, which is the thing that makes a dragon a dragon. If we do not escape this whirlpool, this shark-dragon will eat us. Shark-dragons are not evil but are driven by their hunger. They cannot be reasoned with.

Then we have to get away! Lance thought back. All around them was darkness, and the only thing Lance could see was the shark-dragon as it drew them in. They were trapped.

Can you shoot fire at it?

I have been trying. The Deep Dark quenches my fire. I am sorry, Lance. I should not have brought you down here.

The resignation and sadness flowing from Infinity galvanized Lance into action. If she was too afraid, he would be brave for them both.

No! We can't give up! We are not going to let this thing stop us! We are going to defeat it and find the star! You are the Infinite dragon and I'm . . . Lance's thoughts trailed off, as he tried to think of who he was becoming since he had come to Camp Claw, and more important, who he needed to be in this very moment.

You are my heart-bonded human, Infinity replied. *And together, we can do anything.*

In the dark, Lance grinned. *Exactly.* Through their bond, Lance sensed Infinity regain her hope, and her energy, and she began to thrash in earnest against the pull of the whirlpool created by the shark-dragon's tail.

Holding on to Infinity with just his legs, Lance reached behind him and took out his erhu. He began to play his own song, a song of defense, and to his relief, the music was audible in the water. It was muffled and garbled, but it was there. Slowly but surely the whirlpool began to lose its grip on them.

It's working!

Keep playing and stay focused! Infinity thought back.

But then, just as they were about to break out of the swirling whirlpool, the shark-dragon opened its mouth. There was a pull even stronger than the whirlpool, as if by opening its mouth the shark-dragon had created a vacuum.

Infinity! Lance cried through their bond. He couldn't play his erhu—he could barely hold on to the bow. It felt as if the vacuum coming from the mouth of the shark-dragon was going to rip it out of his hands.

Hold on! Infinity began to tremble with effort, trying to escape the pull, but it was too late. A moment later Lance and Infinity were sucked inside the huge shark-dragon's gaping mouth.

In the Belly of the Beast

Lance let out a cry as the jaws of the shark-dragon closed around them. The teeth came so close, he could have touched one, when suddenly Infinity's horns began to glow gold.

As the teeth were about to crush Lance, a golden bubble erupted from Infinity's horns, enveloping her and Lance within it.

The shark-dragon's teeth clamped down on the bubble and bounced off. The shark-dragon let out a guttural roar that shook the golden bubble, but its teeth still could not pierce it. The creature roared and tried again, but it was as if an extra-strong tennis ball were caught between the jaws of a dog, and the bubble kept the shark-dragon's mouth propped open.

"Come on, you big shark head, spit us out!" cried Lance. To Lance's surprise his voice rang out in the bubble Infinity had created, and he realized he could speak and hear within the bubble, even though it was still filled with water.

But the shark-dragon did not spit them out. Instead, it made a gurgling sound that might have been a laugh, and threw its head back.

The golden bubble, with Lance and Infinity still inside, slid down the shark-dragon's gullet. Lance was more shocked than afraid, and it all happened so fast that by the time he processed the fact that the shark-dragon was swallowing them whole, they were already halfway down to its stomach. As the bubble rolled, Lance and Infinity were tossed around like clothes in a washing machine, round and round, until the golden bubble landed with an audible thud somewhere in the shark-dragon's giant stomach.

Because the shark-dragon was translucent and its tail-light was still glowing, Lance could see through the shark-dragon and into the fathomless depths of the Deep Dark. He could also see exactly where they were in its body.

"How did that happen?" he exclaimed, gently pushing at the interior of the golden bubble. "Did you know you could do that?"

Infinity shook her head, her horns still faintly glowing. "I have never done that before. I do not even know how I did it! I was just focusing on trying to protect you, and pop! The bubble appeared."

"I wish you had known how to do it before we came in the Deep Dark," said Lance. "Would have been useful for getting down here."

Infinity wrinkled her snout. "You know I am still learning how to control my golden elixir! Even when I use it, there can be unexpected results."

"How come I can see the golden bubble? And your horns?"

"Because we are inside the shark-dragon now, and its skin is protecting us from the power of the Deep Dark. I told you, because the shark-dragon was hatched here, it has evolved to thrive in the Deep Dark."

"What else is down here?" Lance gazed into the inky liquid beyond, trying to see anything.

"More monsters than I could count. Many creatures of the dark have made their home here, but they do not bother the rest of Dragon's Claw, or even the rest of the world. Instead, they stay here, waiting for prey to wander in. It is not a safe place, which is why recruits are not allowed in. But sometimes, we find allies in the deep." Infinity thwacked her tail against the side of the golden bubble. "However, the shark-dragon is not an ally. As you can tell since it tried to eat us."

"How are we going to get out of here?" said Lance. "We can't stay inside this bubble, inside this shark-dragon, forever! The others are waiting for us! The star is waiting for us! And we need to rescue the Dragon Force!"

"We will get out," said Infinity. "We just need to figure out a way."

"I think the only way out is *through*." Lance's voice was steely with resolve. "This shark-dragon swallowed us and intends to make us its meal one way or another, and we can't let that happen."

He eyed Infinity's wings, which were currently flat

against her body. "The edges of your wings are quite sharp, right?"

Infinity nodded.

"You know how you can shift colors ... what if you could do more than that? Do you think if you focused, you could shift other things, such as make your wings sharper?"

Infinity's eyes widened. "I have never tried that, but I suppose I could."

Lance swallowed. "Sharp enough to cut our way out of here?"

"Through the skin of the shark-dragon? That ... might work."

"I think it is our only way out," said Lance.

Lance and Infinity sat for a moment in silence, and then the shark-dragon's stomach began to rumble and roil, and something covered in scales that had been chewed up landed on top of the golden bubble. It was unclear what the creature had been before the shark-dragon ate it.

"Right. That settles it," said Lance, dusting his hands off and managing to stand up in the bubble. "We need to get out of here and fast."

Infinity closed her eyes; her horns glowed gold, and Lance saw the edges of her wings sharpen to razor-fine points. "Be careful," she said as she opened her eyes. "I do not want to cut you. I do not know how sharp I have made them."

"Exactly as sharp as they should be," said Lance approvingly.

"If you get on my back and hold on tight, I should be able to angle a wing to use it as a blade, and..." Infinity trailed off.

"And save us," said Lance firmly. He didn't relish the idea of slicing through the belly of the shark-dragon, but it was the only way out—the only way they could survive.

"It shouldn't have swallowed us," said Infinity. "It knew we were still alive, and it still swallowed us."

"It probably didn't think we would stay alive. But that is not our fault," said Lance, carefully climbing into his usual spot on Infinity's back. "Are you ready?"

"I will go through this bubble first, and then through the shark-dragon, and then we will be back in the Deep Dark. And it will be, well, it will be dark again without the shark-dragon's light."

"I would rather be in the dark than in the belly of a shark-dragon."

"A very good point." Infinity readied herself, and Lance felt her tense. And then she leaped up from the bottom of the golden bubble, and with her wing straight out, like a blade, she punctured the bubble.

For one brief moment they were in the belly of the beast, and Lance was overwhelmed by the stench. Infinity kept moving, and her razor-sharp wing soon sliced through the thick translucent skin of the shark-dragon.

As they burst out of its side, the shark-dragon let out a screech that reverberated in the water, and then it went limp.

Infinity, watch out! Lance steered them away just in time. The creature's massive tail swung down in front of them as the shark-dragon pinwheeled down into the depths. When the light on its tail went out, Lance and Infinity were plunged back into darkness.

For a moment they floated in the still silence, and Lance found the darkness strangely soothing.

Are you okay? He could feel Infinity trembling

slightly. He didn't blame her. His head was spinning from what had just happened.

I am glad we are alive, Infinity thought back.

Me too. Lance focused on his bond with Infinity and tried to channel calmness toward her. She must have sensed it because he felt a rush of warmth and affection from her. *You did a great job, Infinity.*

Thank you, Lance.

Lance tried to listen for the song of the star, but he could no longer hear it. *Do you think the star is still down here?*

It must be. Once a star has fallen, it does not rise again. We will find it. Somewhere here in the Deep Dark.

Guilt prickled at Lance. It was his fault that they had been caught by the shark-dragon, his fault they still had not found the star. *I'm sorry I fell for the shark-dragon's trap. If I hadn't been so hasty, if I had listened to you, we probably would have already found the star by now.*

Lance, that was not your fault. You thought it was the star. But . . .

Lance could tell that Infinity wanted to tell him something but was worried it would hurt his feelings.

You can tell me, he reassured her.

But this is only the start of our journey to rescue the Dragon Force. You must trust your instincts, but also be on your guard so you are not so easily tricked. Listen to your heart and your head, and you will not be led astray again.

Lance hung his head, glad that his dragon could not see his shame.

It is a lot to ask of you, Infinity went on. *And we are both young, but I believe we can master our skills, master ourselves, to be the best dragon and human we can be. That is the only way we will ever win against the Devourer and save the others.*

I'll be more focused. I won't be tricked again. But... right now I don't even know how we will find the star. I can't hear it. The song has gone silent.

Play your erhu. The star will hear it and will sing back. Just as it did in the sky. The star would not have fallen unless it was important for us to find it.

It is hard to play in the Deep Dark, Lance admitted.

Close your eyes, Infinity suggested. *Then it will not feel as if you are playing in the dark.*

So Lance did. He swung his erhu around so he

could play it, and closed his eyes. It was still difficult, because the inky water of the Deep Dark was so thick, but he played anyway. He sent out a song of searching, a song that asked for an answer.

And then the answer came. Lance heard the song of the star loud and clear, and he let it wash over him.

I knew we would find the song again. I never doubted you, Lance, Infinity told him through their bond. He could feel her pride, and her joy, at his success, and it made him feel as if he could do anything.

Lance slung his erhu around to his back again. *Come on, Infinity. Let's follow that music and find that star!*

The Starlight Dragon

Lance and Infinity swam through the Deep Dark, following the song of the star.

The song grew louder, and clearer, and Lance knew that they were close.

Then he saw it. And he wondered how he ever could have thought that the flickering light on the end of the shark-dragon's tail was the star.

The star's light was so bright and so beautiful that it felt like looking at hope itself. It shone in the endless dark, calling to Lance and Infinity.

We found it, he thought, relief surging through him. *We found the star.*

As they approached it and Lance shielded his eyes from its brightness, the song grew quieter.

How will we speak to it? Lance wondered to Infinity.

I have never spoken to a star, Infinity thought back. *I do not know what will happen. But stars have ways. It will not have fallen all this way unless it had a plan. Perhaps you should play your erhu again. It seems to respond to that.*

They paused a respectful distance from the star, and Lance tentatively began to play.

In response, the star began to glow even brighter, and then, suddenly, it shattered into thousands of shining fragments. To Lance's amazement, the shimmering fragments reformed into the shape of a dragon.

This star was the spirit of a dragon. Lance could feel Infinity's awe, and it matched his own.

The Starlight Dragon stretched and shifted, until it turned its head to gaze upon Lance and Infinity. It was the only light anywhere that Lance could see.

And when it spoke, he heard it in his mind, the way he heard Infinity.

Hello, little Infinite Dragon. Hello, little Lance Lo.

Lance bristled slightly at being called little, but

then he supposed that to a dragon, he *was* little. And especially to an ancient spirit of a dragon who has been living as a star.

I heard your call, and I came. We stars have watched what has been happening in this strange New World, and we are worried.

I'm worried too, Lance answered.

As you should be. There are things that even the stars fear, and those things are coming. It has been a long time since I have been a dragon—my spirit turned into a star centuries ago—but I still have a dragon heart. I still want what is best for the dragons. And you, Lance Lo—I can tell that you do as well.

And as for you, Infinite Dragon, your time is coming. You must be prepared to do what is asked of you. You must remember that you are the one who can save humans and dragons. This is no false prophecy. The stars have long been waiting for your arrival.

And I know your mother, little Infinite Dragon. All dragon spirits who turn into stars know one another. If she could have, she would have fallen from her place in the sky to speak to you herself, but only the most ancient stars, such as me, can shake free from the sky. One day, though, you will see her again. For her love stretches across time and realms.

Lance felt Infinity's pride and sorrow and love all mingling together at the Starlight Dragon's words. He remembered Infinity telling him that her mother had died in battle when she was still in her egg, and Infinity had been raised by a group of dragons known as the Diamond Clan. Until one day, the Diamond Clan had mysteriously disappeared, and then Infinity had kept herself hidden on Dragon's Claw, the only place that truly felt like home to her, until Lance had arrived. And then she had come out of hiding to find her heart-bonded human. Now she was hearing that she wasn't alone after all. That her mother was a star, and that she was watching over her.

The Starlight Dragon kept speaking. *All the stars believe in you, little Lance and little Infinite Dragon. I would not have sacrificed my place in the sky to come down to these depths if I did not believe that you two, along with your friends, are the key to defeating the Devourer.*

We have long sensed his arrival. Even before the Dragon Realm fell on the Human Realm, there has been a sense in the skies that something else is coming. Something that can destroy us all.

And so we began to sing our song of warning. You, little Infinite Dragon, heard it. And then, lo and behold, as the humans say, Lance Lo heard it too.

Did . . . this ancient Starlight Dragon just make a pun? Lance asked Infinity incredulously.

I did indeed, the Starlight Dragon responded before Infinity could. *And do not look so surprised. I can read every thought in your mind that you have and have ever had. Do not try to hide any thoughts or feelings—it is impossible. And in my long existence, I have seen the thoughts of so many humans, so many dragons. But you two will be the last I speak to. I cannot return to my home in the sky. After this, I will scatter again, and where my spirit will go, I do not know. That is something unknown even to the stars.*

Tears prickled at the back of Lance's eyes as he realized the extent of the star's sacrifice.

Do not let my sacrifice, my journey into the unknown, be in vain. I will tell you now what the stars have seen.

The knowledge we've gained from our vantage point high in the sky. We see all.

The Starlight Dragon gazed directly at Lance, and he felt as if it was looking into his very soul.

We know where the so-called Petrifiers have taken the Dragon Force. Where the Devourer is heading. He is slow, but he is coming. And he has been preparing. This might seem sudden to humans, but not to those of us who have the gift of time. He has long been sending his minions ahead to sow discontent. He sought out those with cruel hearts, such as that man turned beetle. And he has been building a den.

A den? Lance burst out in surprise. The word "den" conjured foxes and cozy forts in his head.

A den. A place where the Devourer can rest after his long journey across the cosmos. And this den, the Devourer's Den, is where his Petrifiers will have brought the Dragon Force. Where they will be keeping all that power for the Devourer to feast on when he arrives.

Well, where is the den? Lance wanted to zoom out of the Deep Dark and go straight to the Devourer's Den.

Do not be so hasty, little Lance Lo. And Lance

remembered how Infinity had just told him the same thing—that he needed to think before leaping into action. *Simply knowing where the Devourer's Den is will not be enough to invade it. It is very cleverly hidden.*

The den itself is made of rocks and bones and ice, floating high in the sky. Not as high as the stars, but hidden among the clouds. I do not know how a human can survive such heights, where the air is so thin, but I also never thought a human could survive the depths of the Deep Dark. You will need dragon magic, but more than that, you will need courage. And wits. Because the Devourer's Den is hidden in plain sight. It is protected by a cloud of poisonous gas. The Devourer and the Petrifiers are immune to it, but it will confuse anyone else. Even dragons. But if you are able to make your way through the mist maze, in the center you will find the Devourer's Den itself. And that is where you will find the Dragon Force.

So it is impossible. Lance tried not to feel dejected, but he couldn't help it.

The Starlight Dragon reared up and snarled at Lance, and he jerked back in fear.

Have you not been listening to what I have been saying? You and Infinity are the key. Do not give up. Conquer your fear. Use your wits! It will be hard. You might die. But if you survive, and you do defeat the Devourer, you will have saved all of human and dragon kind. This is bigger than saving the Dragon Force, little Lance Lo.

I see in your heart you have yearned to be a hero—well, here is your chance. Take it. Do not disappoint me. Do not disappoint your dragon. Do not disappoint yourself. You can do this. You have a dragon on your side. Not just any dragon. The Infinite Dragon. Do not fear your destiny. Embrace it.

Lance wanted to believe the Starlight Dragon's words, wanted to live up to what it was asking. But he still felt so overwhelmed. *How will we even find it if it is hidden in the sky?*

Little Lance Lo, you must be prepared. Do not seek the den until you are ready to defeat the Petrifiers. And then, when you are ready to go to the den, play your erhu. The stars will hear your call, and their song will guide you to the cloud. From the outside it will appear as a storm cloud, but once you pass through it, you will see it for what it is. Survive the poison mist, make your way through the maze, and you will find the Devourer's Den. The stars wish they could do more, but all we can do is guide you with our song, and watch from above.

One of the starlight fragments from the end of the Starlight Dragon's tail began to drift away into the Deep Dark.

I am running out of time. Once a star falls and takes on their dragon spirit form, they do not last long. I will turn into yet another form, one that is a mystery to me.

The Starlight Dragon turned to Infinity. *Do not forget what I have said. Do not forget your own destiny. You must master your own magic to achieve your true greatness. With your human, with Lance Lo, you can do it. Be the Infinite Dragon you are meant to be.*

Then the Starlight Dragon touched its shimmering nose to Infinity's own.

All dragons live forever in one way or another. Make your infinity count.

I will leave you with one last gift, little Lance Lo. Hold out your left hand. The Starlight Dragon flicked its tail toward him, and a piece of starlight drifted in his direction, landing in his outstretched hand.

Lance watched in awe as it melted into his palm, and for a moment his whole body lit up brightly enough to shine even in the Deep Dark. It faded after a moment, leaving only a small shining starburst scar on his left palm.

You now have a tiny piece of starlight with you, wherever you go. To summon it, use your music. Your erhu or your own song. And when you play your erhu, the stars will recognize that someone gifted with starlight is calling, and they will answer.

Fragments of the Starlight Dragon were floating away into the Deep Dark, and Lance realized that soon it would be entirely gone.

Goodbye, Lance Lo. Goodbye, Infinity. May we meet again one day, in one form or another.

And then the Starlight Dragon began to sing again, and Lance knew it was a song of goodbye. With a final blast of light, the Starlight Dragon shattered entirely. For a moment the entire Deep Dark lit up with starlight. In that instant, Lance saw hundreds of creatures all around him that had been hidden in the dark but drawn to the Starlight Dragon. Some with spiky tentacles and one with hundreds of eyes and another that was made entirely of claws. Lance hoped that none of them would come closer to him and Infinity, as he had no interest in getting to know more strange Deep Dark creatures.

When the darkness returned, the only bit of light left was the tiny starburst scar on Lance's palm. He closed his fist so it didn't attract any other creatures, and he and Infinity were plunged back into complete and utter dark.

He knew now, though, that they were not alone—far from it. He had glimpsed how many Deep Dark creatures had come close, from curiosity or hunger, and he did not want to stick around to find out what they wanted.

Infinity, do you know the way back to the surface?
I think so. Hold on!

With a whoosh, Infinity shot upward, and Lance could have sworn he felt a tentacle of *something* brush his cheek. But then it was gone, and he and Infinity were making their way through the Deep Dark, and Lance couldn't wait to feel the true air on his face, to be able to breathe real air. Suddenly they burst out of the Deep Dark, and his friends and his sister were there and they were all laughing and cheering and Lance clutched his fist to his heart and whispered thank you, hoping that wherever the Starlight Dragon was now, it had heard him.

10

Made of Molecule Magic

Lance knew he would never forget the farewell song of the Starlight Dragon, and that it would play in his heart all his life.

It had been a song of hope, and joy, and sacrifice, and bravery—and as the star had shattered, Lance felt every moment of its long life wash over him.

They told the others what they had learned from the star, and when they were done, everyone sat back in awe. They were still on the banks of the Deep Dark, where the rest of the group had been waiting for them to emerge. Bea said that when the whole of the Deep Dark had lit up, they'd been worried and on the brink of sending in another pair to find

Lance and Infinity. "I don't believe you spoke to a star," said Zoe. "That is amazing!"

"Do you think the star really knew my mother?" Infinity's voice was quiet.

"Of course it did," Lance replied, stroking Infinity behind her horns. "Your mother saved us by sending that star on her behalf. They both saved humanity and dragonkind because now we know where we have to go to stop the Devourer."

"The falling star gave us a great gift," rumbled Neon. "We must not squander it."

"Which is why we need to go to the Devourer's Den right away," said Zoe, tilting her head up to gaze at the sky. "Lance, your music and Arthur's pathfinding skills will guide us."

"Zoe, didn't you hear anything Lance just said? We aren't ready!" said Bea. "We need to find the antidote to being petrified! Even the star said that!"

"Zoe, I know how you feel," Lance said. "I want to go as soon as possible too. But we aren't ready yet. We need a plan. The eight of us are strong, but we'll need all of the Dragon Force to defeat the Devourer."

Zoe stamped her feet petulantly. "But we are running out of time! I want to go now!"

"Zoe," said Arthur, coming up and standing in front of her. "What is the point of rushing up to the Devourer's Den just to be petrified ourselves? We have to prepare."

Zoe glowered at him. "Since when were you so practical?"

Arthur smirked. "Since our lives literally depended on it."

Lance laughed as Zoe continued to scowl at Arthur. "Arthur is right, Zoe. You know we need a plan."

Zoe took a deep breath and crossed her arms. "Fine. We can come up with a plan first."

"We need to do things one step at a time," said Lance. He looked at the rest of the group. The sun was just starting to rise, giving them all an almost golden glow. "The star said that the den is hidden in a floating maze of mist and rock and bones—the mist is meant to confuse us, but luckily we can protect ourselves with our own mist."

"I suppose that is my job," said Violet with a whip of her tail.

"Exactly," said Lance. "Instead of your mystifying mist, you can demystify!"

"I have never tried such a thing, but I suppose it is possible," mused Violet.

"Of course it is possible," said Zoe. "You can do anything, Violet!"

Violet nuzzled Zoe with her head. "Especially with you as my human, Zoe. I did not know a human could be so enthusiastic. Or that I would enjoy the enthusiasm quite so much."

"Okay, so we know how we are going to get to the den, but what do we do when we get there?" said Bea.

"We unpetrify everyone," said Lance.

Bea laughed. "Just like that?" She snapped her fingers. "Ta-da! Unpetrified?"

Lance felt his cheeks flush. "Well, not exactly. There has to be an antidote, right? Some magical healing ... thing?" He found himself glancing in Kronos's direction, who was still petrified, with his mouth open, in the center of the Palm. "They won't all stay like that forever, right?"

"Can't golden elixir fix it?" said Zoe.

Infinity shook her head. "Golden elixir imbues

power and magic, but I do not think it can be used to heal. It is too unpredictable."

"The Devourer and his Petrifiers come from another galaxy," said Neon. "They have powers that we have never encountered."

"But Dragon's Claw is the most magical of all places!" Lance burst out. "There has to be something here!"

"I know Dragon's Claw better than anyone," said Infinity softly. "What we seek is not here."

Jaws looked at Violet. "You used to live on Dracordia. Perhaps there you came across something that might be helpful? Especially because you are a healer dragon."

"Dracordia is vast," said Violet. "Much of it I never explored. And even though I am a healer, the Petrifiers are a mystery to me."

"You know who might know about the Petrifiers?" said Arthur. His eyes had taken on a strange, hard look. "Or at least about the Devourer?"

The group all looked at him expectantly. Arthur let out a long breath.

"The Swarm."

*

Nobody liked the idea of going to talk to the Swarm, but Lance couldn't deny that it was the best bet they had of finding out more about the Devourer and the Petrifiers. After all, the Swarm had said he'd been in contact with the Devourer at some point.

It made Lance a little nervous—the thought of talking to the Swarm. Even though the Swarm was now tiny and trapped in a bottle, he had nearly killed them all. What made him the most nervous was the way Arthur's face had looked when he brought up the Swarm. Lance knew that the Swarm had killed Arthur's father and tricked Arthur into weakening the Dragon Force defenses. There was an anger there, bubbling under the surface, and Lance wasn't sure how his friend would react when he came face-to-face with his enemy. But he couldn't deny that it was the best option they had left.

"We should go right away," he said.

"Then it is decided," said Jaws. "To the Labs!"

Everyone climbed astride their dragons. They took off into the sky, in the direction of the Labs, which were just on the other side of the Deep Dark.

As they flew, an alarm began to ring out from the top of the Dragon Force Tower. The alarm blared and lights flashed.

"Um, does that mean something is about to attack Dragon's Claw?" cried Arthur.

Lance inhaled sharply as he stared at the flashing lights. How could the eight of them survive an attack on Dragon's Claw?

"That is one of the alarms for the New World," Jaws replied. "Someone is asking for the Dragon Force's help."

Lance's stomach dropped. "And the Dragon Force isn't here."

Then another alarm went off. "And that is another distress signal," said Neon, starting to sound worried.

"Aren't there Dragon Force members out in the New World?" said Bea.

"Yes ... but when the threat is too big or too dangerous, they call the core Dragon Force team," Jaws explained.

Lance remembered how before the Dragon Force had been captured by the Petrifiers, alarms had started to go off at an increasing rate, calling the elite team away. He wondered what was happening in the New World that was making so many alarms sound.

"We will investigate the calls for help after we talk to the Swarm," said Neon. "Now, everyone, dismount and follow me."

Neon led the group through the Labs. The Labs was an enormous glass, steel, and stone complex that was big enough for dragons to comfortably fly through. As Neon led them down a long corridor, colorful lights shone overhead and unattended gadgets whirred and buzzed on tabletops around them as if they had lives of their own.

"What are those suits over there?" Bea asked, pointing at a dozen or so gray suits, each with the Dragon Force emblem on the chest. The suits were floating in the air behind a glass cabinet. They looked similar to the Dragon Force suit that Lance was wearing, before his had turned orange and gold to match his heart-bonded dragon. But these floating suits were shimmering beneath the lights of the Labs, almost pulsing. "They are full of molecule magic," Bea went on. "I can sense it!"

Neon puffed a plume of smoke from his nostrils as if letting out a sigh. "Those were meant to be the next generation of Dragon Force suits. As you will remember from your training, we have a small amount of golden elixir at the Labs, and it was agreed that tiny traces of this should be used to try to create an even more advanced super-suit for the members of the Dragon Force, stronger and more protective than any suit we've made before. But more than that, the team was trying to use molecule magic to harness the power of the golden elixir to boost the wearer's ability. To make them stronger, faster, more agile. The suit would give you faster reflexes, and even give you the ability to fly in short bursts. Not nearly as fast as a dragon, of course, but if one were to fall off their dragon in battle, they wouldn't plummet to their death. But even with our vast dragon knowledge and advanced molecule magic, we could not get it quite right. There are still too many unknowns about golden elixir. At least for now." Neon let out another huff and started back down the corridor. "This way to the Swarm."

"Wait," said Bea. "Can I take a closer look at the suits?"

Arthur scoffed. "A giant devourer is heading toward us, and the leaders of the Dragon Force have been captured. I don't think we have any time to waste."

Bea waved absently at Arthur, her eyes fixed on the suits. "Just trust me. This is going to sound weird, but I feel as if the suits are calling me." She stepped toward the suits and opened the glass cabinet. She pulled a floating suit from its place and ran her fingers across its surface—first the arms, and then the chest and shoulders, and finally along the back. Her fingertips glowed a faint green and moved with purpose. Lance could tell she was using her powers to examine the suit.

She flexed her fingers outward, and the suit burst into thousands of pieces that lingered in the air, like a snapshot of something mid-explosion. Bea swirled her hands, and the pieces began to swirl as well. Slow at first, and then faster and faster until a small vortex formed in front of them, flashing with green lightning and whirling in place as if captured in a bottle. Bea lowered her hands, her fingertips still glowing, but the vortex kept spinning. She leaned in, and with short finger flicks, she struck flecks out of the vortex, discarding them and letting them fall to the ground.

She moved closer, so near now that her nose was practically in the vortex, and she smirked, her dimple on her right cheek showing. "Just one last tweak." She flicked her fingers again and a small particle shot out, landing by Lance's feet.

"Perfect," she said, placing an open hand at the base of the vortex. She raised her other hand over the vortex and clapped her hands together, smothering it between her hands. The air in the room was still again.

Bea turned toward Lance and revealed a small oblong stone in her hands, the same pearlescent gray color that the suit had been.

Lance trusted Bea, but he didn't like surprises. "What is it?"

Bea huffed. "Just take it."

Lance did as he was told. For the most part, the stone that had come from the suit looked ordinary. Its surface was smooth like an egg and now, looking closer, Lance could see flecks of gold in it. "Now what?"

"Blow on it," said Bea, her dimple still showing. "As if you're blowing out a candle on a birthday cake."

"Is he supposed to make a wish, too?" said Arthur with a scoff, but he was watching closely.

"Come on, Lance," said Zoe, clapping her hands. "I want to see what happens!"

Feeling a little bit silly, Lance took a deep breath and blew on the stone. As his breath hit it, the stone lit up like an ember. Orange-and-gold swirls burst from within the stone like fire caught in a snow globe, but it was still cool to the touch. "Whoa. That is awesome . . ." His voice trailed off. "But other than being a color-changing stone, what does it do?"

Bea's smile widened. "Now close your fist around it."

Lance wrapped his fingers around the stone in his hand and gave it a gentle squeeze. To his surprise, the stone burst like a bubble, releasing a swirling torrent of orange-and-red smoke. For a moment Lance was surrounded by the smoke, and a blink of an eye later, the stone and the smoke were gone.

"Whoa!" cried Zoe, jumping up and down. "That was amazing! You're wearing a new super-suit! How did you do that?"

Lance felt a boost of energy thrumming through his limbs. "I don't know but ... I *feel* amazing. As if I could do anything!" Lance looked down and gasped. His suit was covered in flickering flames, which gave him such a shock that he jumped into the air. To Lance's great surprise, he went so high that he could have leaped over a building. Lance floundered in the air, trying to regain his balance, and he was once again surprised to find that he could effortlessly control his movements. He could twist and turn and cut through the air with ease. It was almost as if he could fly. Or at the very least, it was controlled falling. He did two backflips and landed on the ground with the grace of a seasoned acrobat.

"Truly incredible," said Neon. "I knew you were gifted, Bea, but this is extraordinary. I've never seen any human, or dragon, manipulate molecule magic to this extent."

"Why, thank you," Bea said with a bow. "To be honest, I wasn't sure it would completely work. It's hard to explain, but it was as if I could see exactly what the suit was made of. It was as if the molecules were my friends. I could see them, tell them where to go, and make them work together to create exactly what I wanted. I guess it's kind of like an artist creating a painting, except instead of using paint, I'm using molecules. I could even make out the traces of golden elixir that really supercharged everything." Bea turned to Lance, examining his suit. "And somehow it really worked!"

"You're the greatest scientist who's ever existed," said Zoe, still bouncing with excitement. "I bet they'll make a statue of you somewhere one day."

Bea laughed. "Well, when we save all of the New World together, they'll make statues of *all* of us." She turned back toward Lance. "And don't worry, those aren't real flames on your suit. They just look real."

In all the excitement, Lance had forgotten why he had jumped up in the air in the first place. He looked back down and saw the fabric of his suit was still swirling with orange-and-red flames.

"The fabric can dynamically change colors," Bea continued. "Think of it like a really, really advanced TV screen. When you blew on the stone, the supersuit took in some of your essence and customized itself to be a perfect fit for you. The fabric must look like golden fire because of your bond with Infinity."

Lance looked down at his suit again. "This is amazing! I love it!"

Bea's eyes twinkled. "Just wait until you see what else it can do." She held her finger in the air. "But first, let me make all of our suits."

Bea walked back to the suits and promptly exploded one, swirled it into a vortex, and flicked out the unwanted particles, before turning it to stone. She repeated this twice more and walked back over to the group, three stones in hand.

"One for you," she said, placing a stone in Zoe's hand.

She tossed a stone at Arthur, who caught it coolly in one hand. "One for Arthur."

Bea held out the last stone in her palm and blew on it. The stone turned completely transparent, then lit up with green electricity from within. "And one for me."

Zoe blew on hers, and the stone hopped up and down in her hand. Once. Twice. And then it burst into shifting shades of purple like an avalanche of flower petals falling through the sky on a windy day.

Arthur grinned, unable to hide his excitement. He blew on his, and as his breath hit the stone, the air turned into swirls of black and silver, until the entire surface of the stone looked like a thrashing sea of silver and black.

"Squeeze on three?" Zoe asked.

Arthur and Bea nodded.

"One ... Two ... Three."

Clouds of purple, green, and black burst out of the stones, covering Zoe, Bea, and Arthur. The smoke vanished as quickly as it had appeared, revealing the three of them in their new Dragon Force supersuits. Lance couldn't help but think that it looked like some sort of magic trick, which made sense as Bea used molecule magic to make the suits, after all.

"This. Is. AMAZING!" cried Zoe. The color of her suit matched her rock, dazzling shades of purple dancing across her body.

Lance saw that the color of Bea's and Arthur's suits also matched their stones, green electricity jolting across Bea's suit as if trying to escape while gray-and-black tendrils swirled around Arthur's.

Seeing his new friends—his new team—together

in Dragon Force suits made Lance's heart swell. This was what he had always dreamed of. He looked down at his suit and ran his hand over the Dragon Force emblem on his chest. "Does this mean we're officially part of the Dragon Force now?"

Neon inspected the children. "Only Billy Chan and the other leaders of the Dragon Force can approve that, but you have my vote. And with these new suits, you certainly look the part."

"Oh, don't be so stiff," Jaws grumbled. "I say that from this moment forward, you four children are officially Dragon Force members." Jaws exchanged a look with the other dragons. "We can do that, right?"

"It is simple. We will either save the Dragon Force and all of the New World, in which case it would be preposterous to not have inducted these brave children into the Dragon Force," replied Violet. "Or everyone will be eaten by the Devourer, in which case it would not matter that it had been done."

"That's grim," said Arthur. "Even for me."

"Well, I think this is great news," said Zoe. "I've always wanted to be a real Dragon Force member. I mean, *look* at us! With our new super-suits, we'll be unstoppable!" She ran over to a huge metal cabinet and wrapped her arms around its base. "Seriously, I feel as if I can lift *anything*." Before Lance could say anything, Zoe picked up the cabinet and held it over her head, beaming with joy. "What can't we do in these suits?"

Bea chuckled. "Careful, Zoe. You don't want to tire yourself out before we even get started." Bea touched a hand to her glasses, and a green beam shot out of them, striking the cabinet.

Zoe's mouth hung open as Bea lifted the cabinet out of Zoe's hands with the beam and placed it gently down on the ground.

Bea winked. "I may have upgraded my glasses, too."

"Do you have any other tricks we should know about?" Arthur asked.

"Two things, actually," said Bea, her dimple showing again. "First ... everyone, reach back with one hand and pretend you are gripping an invisible hood and pulling it over your head and face."

Bea demonstrated the movement, and as she did, a helmet appeared on her head.

"Cool!" said Zoe, who had already activated her

helmet. "It's as if I have super-vision in this thing. Everything is *so* clear."

Lance followed Bea's instructions and was amazed when he saw what Zoe meant. All the shadows in the lab were brightened. He looked at the cabinet that Zoe and Bea had lifted, and although he couldn't tell what exactly was inside, he could see the size and shape of the cabinet's contents. He looked all the way down the long corridor of the Labs and found he could focus his vision like a telescope. "Bea, there is *definitely* going to be a statue of you somewhere one day."

"You haven't even seen the last trick yet," said Bea. "Suits, camouflage on!"

All of the children disappeared. Lance raised his hands in front of his face, but couldn't see them.

"You've made us invisible!" said Zoe.

"Well, not quite invisible," Bea replied. "The suits can adapt to their surroundings. Think of them like really advanced chameleons."

"Like Infinity!" said Lance, proud of his dragon's chameleon skill.

"It's so weird talking to thin air," said Arthur, and even though Lance couldn't see his face, he could perfectly picture the expression Arthur was making.

"Oh, maybe this will help," Bea replied. "Everyone, grab the air just in front of your chin and pretend you're taking a hood off your head."

As the group followed Bea's instructions, Lance saw his friends' floating heads in front of him.

"It's how you take your helmet off," Bea explained. "And since our heads aren't covered by the suits anymore, they aren't camouflaged."

Arthur shook his head. "I think talking to floating heads might be even weirder than talking to thin air."

"I think you're right," Bea replied. "Suits, camouflage off!"

Lance saw his body reappear beneath him and let out a sigh of relief. "That is going to take some getting used to."

"Bea, you are the smartest human I have ever encountered," said Neon proudly.

"Very well done, Bea," added Jaws. "Truly remarkable. Now, I would love to be here all day testing out these new suits, but I think we should keep going." Jaws paused and smiled, a sight Lance wasn't sure he would ever get used to. "The world is counting on the newest Dragon Force members to save the day."

Neon turned and made his way down the long corridor. "Jaws is right," he said over his shoulder. "Follow me down to the basement. It is time to see the Swarm."

The Mind of the Swarm

The basement of the Labs was surprisingly dark, with only a few flickering lights along the edges. The group was lined up in single file along another long corridor, which was large enough to fit the dragons, but the space still felt cramped. Neon had opened a secret passage in the floor to access the basement that even Jaws didn't know about.

"I cannot believe this basement has been here all this time," he remarked, sniffing around as if he was trying to find more secrets. He grimaced. "And it smells terrible down here."

"Lower your voice," said Neon. "We are close to the Swarm, and we should be on alert in case our suits have not worked as planned."

They turned off the main corridor into a much smaller room. At the back there was a small floating bottle covered in crackling green electricity. As they approached, Lance could see a half-human, half-beetle that he recognized as the Swarm. The top half of the Swarm was human, while the other half was a beetle body. Two large claws protruded from his waist.

Lance was relieved to see that the Swarm was still miniaturized and asleep in the bottle.

Neon's eyes flashed green. "Awaken."

The creature stirred, the sleep spell slowly releasing its grip. "Where am I?"

"Unimportant," Neon replied. "The question that needs to be answered is what do you know about the Petrifiers? The ones that the Devourer sent."

The Swarm stood, his interest piqued. "Well, well, well. That is a great question." The Swarm gingerly reached out one of his beetle claws and touched the inside wall of the bottle. A loud *pop* rang out, and an electric jolt went through the Swarm. The Swarm shook off the shock and looked back at Neon. "One I will happily answer if you set me free."

"No chance," said Lance.

"That is a shame," said the Swarm. "I guess there is also no chance that I tell you how to defeat the Petrifiers and how to unpetrify all your pathetic friends in the Dragon Force."

Lance pulled out his erhu and strummed a low, melodic rhythm like the beat of a heart. "Tell us what you know." He hoped that his song spell would convince the Swarm, almost like hypnosis.

The Swarm let out a chuckle. "Oh, how cute. You think your songs can enchant me? Make me tell you what I know? My mind is unbreakable. Impenetrable. Your only option is to let me be free." The Swarm smiled with his whole face. "I promise I'll be good."

Flushing, Lance returned his erhu behind his back. He had been so sure it would work, and he was embarrassed that the Swarm had mocked him.

Zoe put her hand on Lance's shoulder. "That was a good try." She looked around the group. "Anyone have any other ideas?"

"Do you think we should let him out?" Bea asked tentatively. "It might be a good trade."

"Absolutely not!" Arthur cried. "He can't be trusted! There's no way we can let someone like him be free!"

Bea lowered her voice. "I'm not saying you're wrong, but these are really extreme circumstances. I just think it's worth considering the pros and cons of all our options."

"Pros and cons?" Arthur replied, spit flying from his mouth, his eyes watery. "We're talking about a murderer!"

Jaws stepped forward. "Arthur is right. We cannot let the Swarm out."

"Maybe we should have a vote," Zoe offered.

"I can't believe we're even discussing this!" said Arthur. He was so upset, he turned away from the group. As Lance watched him, he saw Arthur pull an object from his pocket and bring it to his mouth. Lance was shocked to see that it was a vial of golden elixir. Before he could do anything, Arthur had swallowed a droplet. Was he using it to power up? It was so dangerous—what was he thinking? And where had he even found a bottle of the precious substance?

Lance ran to Arthur and grabbed his wrists, but it was too late. "What are you doing, Arthur?"

Arthur pulled his wrists free and turned back to the Swarm, his face hard and determined.

"TELL ME WHAT YOU KNOW."

The Swarm laughed an evil laugh. "Child, you are so naive. Just like your father was."

Arthur raised his palms at the Swarm. "Tell me what you know," Arthur repeated as he shot a rope of gray smoke out from each palm. The ropes of smoke whipped out toward the bottle holding the Swarm and slid through the crackling electricity and glass of the bottle like knives going through butter. The smoke ropes then shot toward the Swarm like snakes and burrowed themselves in the Swarm's ears, one on each side. Lance gasped.

For the first time the Swarm's eyes flashed with concern. "Boy, what are you doing?"

Arthur stared intensely into the Swarm's eyes. "Tell me what you know," he repeated. "Or I will make you show me."

"Your pathetic games won't work with me," the Swarm replied, regaining his composure.

Arthur took a step closer to the Swarm and looped the smoke ropes around his hands, tightening his grip. "Tell me or I will make my way through the maze of your mind until I find what I am looking for." Lance realized that Arthur was using his pathfinding power to search the Swarm's mind, to seek the knowledge that the Swarm was hiding. It was terrifying but brilliant, and Lance hoped his friend never turned on him.

"Arthur, this is intense," said Bea in a low whisper.

Arthur furrowed his brow. "These are intense circumstances, and this is the least bad option. There is no maze that I cannot find my way through." Then he refocused on the Swarm. "I said, SHOW ME."

"*Never*," the Swarm replied, falling to his knees and bringing his beetle claws to his head. "Get out! Get out! Get out of my head! I will never show you!"

Arthur twisted his palms, sending a ripple through the gray ropes. The Swarm shot back up on his beetle legs as if he was being shocked, his head whipping backward.

"There it is," said Arthur, tilting his head slightly to the side as he stared into the Swarm's eyes.

The Swarm shook his head, his mouth trembling as if he were holding back vomit. And then, against his will, he relented. "The antidote for those who have been petrified is the seed of a blood berry." His voice shook as he spoke, fighting to hold in what Arthur was forcing out. "Press the seed into their skin." He paused, still trembling with effort, fighting against Arthur's power.

Arthur whipped the ropes of smoke once more and the Swarm's head recoiled. "To f-fully defeat a Petrifier is t-twofold," he stammered. "First, you must face and conquer your fear, so they cannot use it against you. And then you must reflect a Petrifier's terror back on them, and they themselves will become petrified. You must know that the Petrifiers feast on fear. NOW GET OUT OF MY HEAD."

Arthur twisted his hands again. "Where do we find blood berries?"

"I don't know! My master never told me! He sent a Petrifier to my lair, to test me. But it did not petrify me. I have seen too much to know fear. And the Petrifier told me it had never encountered a creature that it could not petrify. Then I asked it if there was any way for one who had been petrified to be unpetrified, because I was curious. I was once a scientist, after all. And it told me about blood berries, about how they are the only antidote to being petrified. But

I do not know where to find them. Only that they exist and that they are the only thing that can unpetrify a living creature who has been petrified." The Swarm's eyes were bulging now. "Now I know what fear is. And it is this! Having you inside my head!"

"Arthur, let him go," said Lance gently. "We found out what we needed."

Arthur lowered his hands, and the ropes of smoke went slack and dissipated into the air. The Swarm fell to the floor of the bottle. "That was not very nice," he said between heavy breaths. "Although I cannot blame you. I would have done exactly the same thing in your circumstances. I suppose you will leave me here now."

"Finally, something we agree on," said Arthur.

"Let us leave this vermin," said Jaws. And without another word, the group turned and left the basement of the Labs, the Swarm still small and trapped in his bottle.

12

Danger Detected

As they left the basement of the Labs, Lance noticed Neon pausing to put up electric force fields behind them.

"What are you doing?" he asked, eyebrows furrowing with curiosity.

"I do not trust that beetle-man," Neon said simply, directing his focus on a doorway before it lit up in glowing, buzzing green. "Yes, he is trapped in a bottle in which I myself sealed him, but I want to make sure nothing else gets in to release him. I once thought Dragon's Claw was impossible to attack, but nothing is as I once believed. These are strange times."

"Indeed," said Violet, whipping her tail. "Let us get back above ground, where the air is fresh." She shuddered. "I do not like it in here, beneath the Labs. It feels unnatural."

"But some dragons live in mountains or in the sea, right?" asked Bea.

"Yes," said Jaws. "Like humans, all dragons are different. Some might make their homes deep underground, some in the sea, and others prefer to fly in the sky."

"Who would want to be trapped?" said Violet. "To fly is to be free." They came up into the main space of the Labs and then out into the early morning light. Violet zoomed into the air and flew in figure eights and diamonds, making shapes in the sky with her long serpentine body.

"Infinity, you spent a lot of your time inside the Volcano, right?" said Lance, turning to his dragon.

"I felt safe there," said Infinity quietly. "The Diamond Clan, the dragons who raised me from a hatchling, said that when I was an egg, they kept me in a different volcano, one in Dracordia, to keep me warm and protected. I have always liked heat."

"What is the Diamond Clan?" said Zoe. "They sound amazing!"

"And they were," said Jaws. "A group of four dragons who looked like living gemstones. They had incredible powers of the kind I had never seen."

"What happened to them?" asked Arthur.

"They disappeared one day." Infinity's voice was tinged with sadness.

"No one knows where they went. And perhaps one day they will return." Neon sent one more electric blast all over the Labs, which for a moment glowed the same green as his scales, before he turned to assess the group. "But what we must discuss now is Arthur. Arthur, what you did with the golden elixir was—"

"Brilliant!" Zoe burst in. "How did you *do* that? You went *into* his brain! It was so cool!"

"I was going to say 'reckless,'" said Neon, his voice stern. "Golden elixir is incredibly dangerous and incredibly rare."

"But none of us can deny that it got results," said Jaws, gently headbutting Arthur.

"Regardless, we cannot forget that golden elixir

is extremely unpredictable," Neon went on. "It is only to be used with extreme caution. You could have hurt yourself, or injured all of us. If things had gone differently, if your poorly conceived plan had backfired, the Swarm could have escaped—and he could have taken that vial of golden elixir from you. What would have happened then?"

Arthur looked shamefaced. "I wanted to help. I knew it would work, and it did!"

"And so far golden elixir has made everything better!" Zoe spluttered. "Look what it did to our suits!" She twirled around, and the new purple petal design on her suit seemed to flutter in the breeze. And then she hopped into the air and hovered, like a hummingbird. "We can *fly*!"

"You can hover," corrected Violet, gently swatting Zoe on the bottom with her tail so Zoe lost her balance in the air and landed back on the ground with an *oomph*. "But do not get overconfident."

Zoe laughed as she stood and dusted herself off. "Good point."

"The suits are a combination of golden elixir and Bea's skill with molecule magic," said Neon. "And it was only minuscule amounts. And golden elixir is in the material of the suits, not directly ingested by humans."

"Well, what about Arthur? He drank golden elixir, and it made him more powerful! He was able to find a path *into* the Swarm's brain! If he hadn't used it, we probably never would have gotten anything out of the Swarm!" Zoe insisted. "Obviously, golden elixir takes your powers and levels them up!" Her eyes were shining with excitement. "We can definitely defeat the Devourer—Infinity makes golden elixir! We'll be unstoppable!"

"I am still learning how to control my own powers," admitted Infinity. "I do not know if we can depend on my abilities."

"Of course we can depend on you, Infinity," said Lance. He wished Infinity were more confident. None of the other dragons needed as much reassurance, but he supposed none of the others had the kind of powers that Infinity had, or mysterious prophecies about them. "You can create the most powerful substance in all of the galaxy!"

"As I have now said several times," Neon spoke

more loudly now, and Lance felt a little bit as if he was being scolded in school, "golden elixir is incredibly powerful but also incredibly dangerous, and we must only use small amounts. You all saw what happened to the Swarm. Do you think he intended to turn himself into a beetle-man?"

"Probably," muttered Arthur. "Now he is as monstrous on the outside as the inside."

Neon let out a loud harrumph. "We can discuss the appropriate ways to use golden elixir another time. Right now we need to discuss what the Swarm has told us."

"Something he wouldn't have revealed unless I used golden elixir," Arthur quipped.

"Arthur, don't you see? What you did was extremely dangerous. It is lucky that you are okay," Lance said, his frustration showing in his voice. He took a deep breath, trying to calm his nerves. He knew that Arthur had only been trying to help, but it had been very risky, and if they were going to save the Dragon Force and defeat the Devourer, they needed to work as a team.

"I would do it again," Arthur said, eyes flashing. "I don't regret it at all." Lance realized why Arthur had acted so strongly and why he was so angry. The Swarm had killed Arthur's father and deceived Arthur into helping him attack the Dragon Force. And if everything had gone to plan for the Swarm, Arthur would be dead too.

"I think what we're trying to say," said Lance, his voice softer now, "is that we can't do this without you. We need you. And, yes, that was pretty incredible what you did in the Labs. And you're right; we probably wouldn't have gotten that information out of the Swarm without you. But we need you! So just be careful, okay?" Lance gave Arthur a gentle shove with one arm.

Arthur smirked and elbowed Lance in return. "Is this lecture done? Can we get back to the more important job of, oh, saving the world? Using the information I found out?"

Lance raised his eyebrows at Arthur, waiting for him to be even slightly contrite. "You don't have to regret what you did, but you have to be more careful."

Arthur sighed and held his hands up. "Okay, okay! I promise I'll be more careful."

Lance smiled, then turned to address the group.

"Okay," said Lance. "We need a plan. Here is what we know." He held out a hand and counted on his fingers as he spoke. "The first thing is that the stars will show us how to get to the Devourer's Den once we are ready."

"That's right," said Zoe.

"And to be ready," Bea jumped in, "we need to figure out how to defeat the Petrifiers and how to unpetrify everyone that has been petrified."

"Exactly," said Lance, proud that they were working together as a team. "So we know that Petrifiers feast on our fears. That is how they freeze us and turn us into stone. But according to the Swarm, and based on what happened with the Petrifier in the Volcano, if we conquer our fears, their attacks won't work—they won't be able to petrify us."

"But we need to do more than block their attacks," said Arthur. "To truly defeat them, we have to reflect terror back on them, and they themselves will become petrified."

Lance nodded. "Right." He cleared his throat. "Anyone have any ideas for how we can reflect the Petrifiers' attacks back at them?"

There was a pause as the group considered Lance's question.

Zoe's eyes lit up. "Bea, maybe you can make some sort of fear-reflecting mirror with your molecule magic!"

Bea thought about this for a moment, then shook her head. "I don't have any idea how I would do that." She shrugged. "Feelings aren't made of molecules."

"Lance," said Arthur, "maybe you can use your erhu to defeat the Petrifiers like we did with the one in the Volcano?"

Lance shook his head, recalling how hard it'd been to defeat a single Petrifier. "I know I was able to use my erhu to slow down the Petrifier in the Volcano, but I don't think there's any way it would work against an army of them. You heard what the Devourer said—there are as many Petrifiers as there are hairs on his body. An umbrella might work in the rain, but it would collapse under a waterfall. We need something stronger before we go into the Devourer's Den." He paused, chewing on his lip as he thought. "*We* need to be stronger. But how?" He glanced over at the training cubes dotted around the palm of Dragon's Claw. "Is there anything in the training cubes that can help us train our minds instead of our bodies? Help us master our fears?"

"Not in the training cubes," said Infinity quietly. "But there is a place here on Dragon's Claw where your fears can be brought to life in front of you. Where your mind and eyes play tricks on you."

Electricity flickered between Neon's sharp horns. "Infinity, you cannot be suggesting what I think you are." His voice was a low warning. "We have already been too risky with golden elixir. I will not allow the children to risk themselves further."

Suddenly, Lance knew what Infinity was referring to. "The Mirage," he said. "Nothing is as it seems there, right? That sounds like the perfect place to train ourselves to face our fears."

"It is more than that," said Neon. "Dragons and humans can lose sense of everything there. Where they are. Who they are. You can go in and never come out. Or come out completely changed. We are not going into the Mirage, and that is final."

Bea placed a soothing hand on the back of Neon's

neck. "Neon, we make these decisions as a team, remember?"

Lance's mind was whirring. "Hold on. If the Mirage can show us our fears . . . is there something in the Mirage that we can take with us to reflect fear back at the Petrifiers?"

Jaws scoffed. "The Mirage is not a beach you can take a shell from."

But Lance didn't care what Jaws or Neon had to say about the Mirage. They didn't know it like Infinity did. He turned to Infinity. "Infinity?"

"Lance is not wrong," she said after a moment.

"Yes!" Lance exclaimed, pumping his fist in the air. He knew he had been on the right track about the Mirage. Neon glared at him but didn't say anything.

"But Neon is *also* correct," Infinity went on. "The Mirage is a mysterious and dangerous place." Neon let out a satisfied *hmph* that made his long mustache flutter in the air. Lance supposed it was Neon's version of a fist pump.

But Lance wasn't finished with this discussion.

"Infinity, the Mirage isn't dangerous to *you*!" Lance burst out. "You told me you go there all the time."

"You are right. I do have special ties to the Claw and have been to the Mirage many times. In fact, the Mirage is where I found the erhu you wear on your back. It was my first trip into the Mirage, and I was still a hatchling. The Mirage drew me in; it was calling to me. I've not told you this before, but the Mirage is more than a lagoon. It is sentient. It has a consciousness. And when I entered its foggy depths, it gave me a choice. It could see my potential even though I could not, and it made me an offer. It said if I could pass its challenge and prove myself worthy, it would allow me in and out of its depths whenever I liked. But if I failed the challenge it had for me, I would be lost in the Mirage forever. I agreed, and I nearly failed, but I managed to survive and the Mirage kept its word. I now go in and out as I please, and the Mirage hasn't spoken to me since."

"Maybe you can go back and ask it to help us!"

"You misunderstand," said Infinity. "I have tried, many times, to speak to the Mirage again, but it has never replied."

"Maybe if we all go in together!" Lance continued, still holding on to the idea. "The Mirage might make us a deal as well. If we can pass its challenge, then it will help us with the Petrifiers."

"Perhaps," said Infinity, mulling the idea over.

"This sounds like a ridiculous plan to me," said Arthur. "Hope that some cloudy ... essence talks to us? I know I was the one who swallowed golden elixir, but this is next-level foolishness. I don't want to be lost in the Mirage forever!"

"What other options do we have?" Lance asked.

"It just seems like a huge risk to take," said Arthur.

"Okay, before we get too heated about this, because I can tell there are some strong feelings here," said Bea, interjecting, "let's just say we do all go into the Mirage as Lance is suggesting and somehow manage to get the Mirage to help us, we still need to figure out the *other* thing the Swarm said—how do we get ahold of blood-berry seeds to unpetrify the Dragon Force?"

"I fear that task may be even harder than fighting the Petrifiers," murmured Violet, who had been silent during the discussion about the Mirage. "I may not know much about the Mirage here on Camp Claw, but I do know Dracordia, and I have heard rumors of this blood-berry tree. It will be very difficult indeed."

Lance couldn't see how *anything* could be much harder than battling an army of Petrifiers. "What do you—?"

Lance was cut off by the sound of alarms blaring from the Dragon Force Tower. They all froze and gazed up at it.

"What is that?" said Lance, instinctively stepping closer to Infinity.

"We must get to the Dragon Force command center immediately," said Neon, green electricity flickering all over him. "Something is about to attack Dragon's Claw."

An Unexpected Transformation

High in the Dragon Force Tower, the group gathered around the consoles that showed two maps: one was the air space above Dragon's Claw, and the other an entire map of the New World.

Lance could see a strange shape barreling through the sky toward Dragon's Claw.

"How can we see that?" he said, pointing at the shape. "And what is it?"

"Satellites," said Neon. "Human technology has its uses, you know."

"I cannot make out what it is, though," said Neon,

frowning. "It is disrupting our technology somehow."

"We will not know what it is until it is nearly upon us," Jaws added. "Which will make it tricky to prepare for."

Lance switched his attention to the other map—the one of the New World. It was lit up with yellow flashing lights. "And these?" asked Lance.

"Those are attacks in the New World," Jaws said, and his voice was solemn. "I have never seen so many at once."

An awful thought occurred to Lance. "Do you remember when the Devourer spoke through the Petrifier in the Volcano?" Lance himself knew he would never forget how terrifying it had been. How it had been his first glimpse of just how powerful the Devourer was. Then came the knowledge that the Devourer knew about him, and about Infinity.

Everyone nodded.

"One of the things he said was that the Petrifiers are made of his own fur, parts of him that he can shed and send on in advance of his coming."

The group looked expectantly at Lance, waiting for him to get to the point.

Lance gulped. "So isn't it possible that the Devourer sent Petrifiers all over the New World? And the reason these places all need help is because ... there aren't any Dragon Force members there to help them? Because they were all petrified?"

Neon and Jaws went very still. "That ... that would be impossible," said Jaws.

"It would explain all the alarms," said Infinity quietly.

"Isn't there some way to check?" asked Arthur.

"Every active Dragon Force member, human or dragon, has a pendant through which they can be contacted. It is also how they ring the alarm when they need more assistance." Neon shot a blast of electricity at a button on the dashboard, and it lit up.

"THIS IS NEON AT DRAGON CLAW. I NEED ANY DRAGON FORCE MEMBERS WORLDWIDE TO RESPOND. ARE YOU THERE?"

There was a static crackle and then a long beep.

"I REPEAT. DRAGON FORCE MEMBERS. MAKE YOURSELVES KNOWN."

Still there was no response.

"It cannot be," rumbled Jaws. "There are so many of us."

"Less than a thousand," said Arthur. "In the whole world, that isn't very many."

"There are still dragons out there, though," said Bea. "Right?"

"Yes, but any dragons not in the Dragon Force are what the Dragon Force call 'rogue dragons,'" Violet explained. "Ones like me, who do not feel any kind of loyalty to humans or the Dragon Force until they find their own heart-bonded humans. If they ever do."

Zoe grinned at Violet. "So basically, because of me, you don't hate humans?"

"I don't hate *you*," clarified Violet, blowing out a stream of purple-tinged smoke that ruffled Zoe's hair. "I am still undecided on humans as a whole."

"I love all dragons," said Zoe, still beaming at her dragon. "But especially you."

"I think Violet has a point," said Arthur. "I mean, I am undecided on humans as a whole too."

Lance looked at the map that kept lighting up on the dashboard, and a bad feeling settled in the pit of his stomach. "So, all of these areas are in danger, and there aren't any Dragon Force members there to protect them?" What was everyone going to do? What about his parents? "Can we take a look at New London?" His heart felt as if it had a fist around it. The whole world was under attack, including his corner of it. What was the point of being in the Dragon Force if they couldn't save anyone? Panic began to unfurl inside him, and he felt unsteady on his feet.

"New London is under attack," said Jaws after a moment. "I do not know what it is, because we have no Dragon Force members on the ground to report back."

"We have to go!" said Lance. "We have to see what is attacking New London! We have to save them!"

"Lance, the way we save everyone is to unpetrify and free the Dragon Force and stop the Devourer," said Bea gently. "I'm scared for my family too, but I know I can't go rushing back to Argentina. We have to stay focused."

"Mom and Dad will be okay," said Zoe, squeezing his hand. It felt a little strange for his younger sister to comfort him instead of the other way around, but Lance was grateful for it.

"And I suppose those rogue dragons in the New World could possibly be convinced to help protect the humans," admitted Violet. "But there are no guarantees."

Lance snorted. "Is that supposed to be reassuring?"

Violet fixed her unblinking gaze on him. "No. It is supposed to be realistic. You must be prepared to face the hard truths of the world, or you will never be able to face your fears."

"But do not give up hope," added Infinity, coming closer to Lance. "Hope fuels us all. Even dragons."

Lance drew a steadying breath, and as he did, he felt the fist around his heart relax. He forced himself to take another breath, to stay calm. To stay hopeful. "I guess I just have to hope all our families and friends are all right. And all we can do is focus on saving the Dragon Force."

"And to do that, we have to save ourselves from whatever is about to land on Dragon's Claw," said Arthur, pointing at the map that showed the air space over Dragon's Claw. It was true—the strange shape was getting ever closer.

Lance felt shaky and overwhelmed. His throat was

parched. When was the last time any of them had eaten or drunk anything?

"Lance? Are you okay?" Zoe frowned in concern.

"I'm just worried about ... everything," he said. He turned to the dragons. "Do we have any water? Or food? I think we'll have a better chance of facing the Devourer, and whatever that thing is"—he waved in the direction of the map still showing shapes falling toward Dragon's Claw—"if I don't have to do it on an empty stomach."

"I'm glad someone mentioned food," Arthur chimed in. "I'm starving."

"There," said Neon, nodding at a fridge and cupboard at the back of the room. "Dragons, of course, do not need to eat as often as humans, but I have seen Dragon Force members get food from that when they are in here for long periods of time."

"Let's see what we've got," said Arthur, heading over to the fridge. "Water, apples, cheese ..." He pulled open the cupboard. "And brown bread. Pretty basic stuff."

"I'll take it," said Lance. Arthur tossed him an

apple that Lance caught with one hand. He bit into it and almost immediately felt better.

Arthur brought the rest of the food over, and they all tore into it. "Bread has never tasted so good," said Arthur with his mouth full.

"I didn't realize how hungry I was," added Bea.

"Humans. Always needing food," said Jaws with a shake of his head.

It felt strange to sit in the command center of the Dragon Force Tower eating bread and cheese while the alarms continued to blare.

"Okay, now I'm ready," said Bea as she took a swig of water. "I needed that."

Zoe stood and walked over to the map that indicated something was heading toward Dragon's Claw. It was still unclear what it was, which made Lance nervous. He joined his sister, trying to make sense of the shape. Right now it still looked completely theoretical—a blob in the sky.

But he knew there was a reason that the Dragon Force shields had picked up on it.

"That isn't . . . the Devourer, is it?" he said quietly. He wondered if they all had been thinking it. It felt almost unlucky to say it out loud, as if he would summon the creature by saying its name.

"That thing?" said Zoe incredulously, pointing at the blob. "That is a blob. I am not afraid of a blob."

"Do not be fooled by the shape," said Neon. "We will not know what it is until it is nearly upon us."

"We can't just sit here and wait! We have to prepare!" Arthur said, beginning to pace. "Maybe I can use my pathfinding ability to see exactly where it is in the sky, or at least figure out the size of it in the air."

"Oh!" said Infinity. "That gives me an idea! Let me try something." She closed her eyes. A moment later there was a *boom*, and a blast of gold light erupted out of her horns, exploding all around them. As it washed over Lance, he felt a strange tingling sensation. It didn't hurt, but it felt odd.

"Whoa!" said Arthur. "What was that?"

Infinity opened her eyes. "It is not the Devourer," she said.

"How do you know?" asked Lance.

"And did it have anything to do with that gold light you just blasted?" added Bea.

"It was a seeking blast. It does not hurt anyone,

but whoever the golden light touches, I can sense their power levels. And the thing coming toward us is powerful, but not nearly as powerful as what I imagine the Devourer would be," Infinity explained.

"Have you . . . always been able to do that?" asked Lance in awe.

Infinity shook her head. "Much like the bubble I made for us in the Deep Dark, this is something new." She sounded as shocked as Lance felt. Her eyes widened. "I feel as if I am gaining new powers all the time." She stood on her hind legs and opened her paws, gazing down at her claws. "It feels as if the power inside me is bubbling, waiting to erupt." When standing, she was almost over three meters tall.

"Well, I hope that you can use it in battle!" said Arthur. "If you can figure out how to aim that power, you could use it as a way of detecting the weaknesses of our enemies and help us plan our attacks to avoid the most dangerous areas!"

"I will do my best," said Infinity.

"Your powers have always been activated in times of need," mused Neon. "As the Devourer draws closer, you will be growing more powerful."

"Preparing for your destiny," added Jaws.

"While it is a relief to know that it is not the Devourer at our doorstep, something powerful is still coming," said Violet. "We must be ready to fight."

"And I'm ready!" said Zoe, brandishing something in her hand. It glinted gold. "More than ready! I'm going to level up!"

"Zoe, what is that?" said Lance, moving toward his sister, but she was too fast. She whipped out a stopper from the bottle in her hands and poured the contents down her throat.

"Is that more golden elixir?" Lance shouted, incredulous and angry. "Zoe!"

Zoe fell to the ground and began to convulse. Lance dropped down next to her and held her hand. Zoe's eyes rolled back in her head. Lance looked up at Violet in panic. "Violet! Do something!"

Violet flew close to Zoe, her mouth set in a severe line as she inspected her human. "This is beyond my skill as a healer. Golden elixir is not something to be healed from. It is a most dangerous drink, especially for humans. I do not want to interfere and perhaps make it worse."

Zoe was still shaking all over as Lance gripped her hand. "Infinity, you can do something, right?"

"I wish I could," said Infinity, and there was a sadness in her voice. "But golden elixir is already in her system. It would be far too dangerous for me to try to withdraw it. There is no going back now. We must let it take its course."

"She drank so much," said Bea quietly, kneeling down next to Lance and taking Zoe's other hand. "I can sense it in her bloodstream, the same way I could sense it in our suits. Where did she get that bottle of it?"

"She must have taken it from the Labs as well," said Arthur. "I can't believe she drank the whole thing." He let out a long breath. "I only drank a drop and even that felt as if I was swallowing a bomb."

"It is very irresponsible of you both," growled Neon. "We have told you all how powerful it is."

"I did what I had to do," said Arthur defensively. "I got that information out of the Swarm, didn't I? And maybe Zoe has a plan."

"No, she doesn't," said Lance, his gaze still locked

on his sister. "And I bet seeing you drink it gave her the idea to try it."

"Hey!" said Arthur. "Don't blame me! I wasn't the first one to use golden elixir! You used it against the Swarm. And if your sister drank too much golden elixir, that was her choice."

"Stop arguing," ordered Bea. "Right now we need to focus on making sure Zoe is okay."

"She never should have come to Camp Claw," said Lance, his voice trembling. "She was too young!" He tore his gaze away from Zoe's face to glare at Violet. "Why did you bond with her so early?" This had to be someone's fault. And if he couldn't get angry at Arthur, he was going to get angry at Violet. Because deep down, Lance felt as if it was his fault. He should have been watching her more closely; he should have protected his sister. He had failed.

Violet snarled at him. "Watch your tone, human boy. The heart-bond cannot be forced and it cannot be controlled. I found Zoe because she was ready."

"Fine!" snapped Lance. The rational part of his brain told him to stop fighting with a dragon, but the other part of him was too angry to listen to it. "But didn't you sense what she was going to do? Before she did it? Why didn't you stop her from drinking the golden elixir?"

"Dragons cannot control their humans," said Neon. "Just as you cannot control Infinity. You have the bond but, ultimately, we all make our own decisions and must face our own consequences."

"I don't want a philosophy and ethics lesson! I want someone to save my sister!" Lance was shouting now, shouting at all the dragons, but he didn't care. All he cared about was making sure Zoe was safe.

She stopped shaking, suddenly, and went limp, which was even worse.

"Zoe! Zoe!" Lance gripped his sister by the shoulders. Why had she been so reckless? He was incredibly scared and worried, but he was furious, too. How could she have done this? "One of you has to be able to do something!" he screamed at the dragons. What was the point of having a dragon, of having magic, if you couldn't save the people you loved most in the world? "Zoe, wake up!"

She was still breathing; she was still alive. Lance told himself this over and over again, even as strange purple veins began to appear on Zoe's face.

The alarm that had been blaring grew louder and more insistent. "We must prepare for an imminent attack," said Jaws. "Whatever is coming is powerful."

"I'm not leaving my sister," said Lance fiercely.

Suddenly Zoe lifted up into the air with so much force that Lance had to let go of her, and she began to glow. Purple and gold beams of light streamed out of her body, as if she was lit up from the inside and she couldn't contain it.

Lance reached up for her, trying to pull her back down.

Then Zoe's eyes opened wide and she let out a long, terrified scream.

"SOMEONE HELP HER!" Lance shouted. But the air around her was crackling with power, and even Violet couldn't get close. Zoe's back arched and then two purple wings sprouted out below her shoulders, tearing through her super-suit. They looked like giant butterfly wings with sharp edges. A tail came next, growing from the base of her spine at an alarming speed and nearly whacking Arthur in the face. Zoe had stopped screaming now and was staring at her rapidly changing body with an expression of complete shock. As Lance gaped, Zoe's arms curled toward her body, and when they shot back out, instead of hands, she had claws. Then her legs retracted into her and burst out of the super-suit, reemerging as scaly dragon feet, complete with claws.

"Zoe!" Lance yelled out to his sister, desperately wanting to comfort her, to be there for her. He stared hard at her face, trying to memorize it. Because now he knew what was coming next.

With a gasp, Zoe dipped her head down, and her hair covered her face. Lance knew she wasn't in control of her movements—that the golden elixir inside her had taken over and all Zoe could do was wait until it was over. Lance just hoped it didn't hurt.

When Zoe raised her head again, a new face stared out at them.

A dragon's face.

14

A Dragon Double

"Zoe? Is that you?" whispered Lance.

Dragon Zoe dropped down to the floor and landed on all fours. She was still remarkably similar to Zoe in her human form, but with added tail and wings.

Dragon Zoe coughed and then looked directly at Lance.

Lance blinked in surprise, because even though this creature was a dragon, she still resembled Zoe. The eyes weren't dragon eyes, they were Zoe's eyes, just in a dragon's face. The snout even sort of looked like Zoe's nose, except it was purple and had long whiskers, and, well, now she had two small horns protruding out of the top of her head, and a purple mane running from between her horns all the way down her back.

But it was still undeniably *Zoe*.

"Am I a dragon?" said dragon Zoe, and to Lance's relief, she sounded just like his sister. Dragon Zoe did a little twirl, trying to inspect herself, and she looked like a puppy chasing her tail. "I *am* a dragon! Am I dreaming?"

Arthur rubbed his eyes. "Are we all dreaming?"

"Zoe! You are such a cute dragon!" cooed Bea. Then she frowned. "But . . . surely you can turn back into yourself, right?"

"I don't know," said Zoe. "I don't know how I turned into a dragon!"

"Because you drank too much golden elixir," said Neon disapprovingly. "How did you even get so much without us noticing?"

Zoe hung her head and her tail slid between her legs. "After I saw what Arthur was able to do with golden elixir, I secretly replicated myself and sent my replica back into the Labs to find me my own vial of it."

"That was incredibly irresponsible," Neon chided. "And even more irresponsible to drink golden elixir.

Although I have to say, I do not think any of us were expecting . . . this."

"You make a very good dragon," said Violet proudly. "I may even prefer you as a dragon to a human."

"I would like Zoe to be back in her human form, personally," said Lance. He looked expectantly to Infinity. "You can do that, right?"

Infinity dropped down on all fours so she was closer to Zoe. "I . . . will try." She let out another blast of golden light, just as she had done when trying to assess the power of the incoming attack.

"She feels like a dragon," said Infinity after a moment. "But her heart is a human heart. And her mind is too. But her powers . . . they are dragon powers."

"Cool!" said Zoe, blowing out a small experimental puff of air. All that came out was smoke. It was brighter than Violet's lavender smoke—more of an electric purple. "Aw! I thought I would be able to breathe fire!" She tried again, and this time a small purple flame flickered to life.

"Careful!" said Lance, moving out of the way. "Zoe! This isn't a joke! You turned yourself into a dragon!"

"I know! Isn't it *awesome*?" crowed Zoe.

"No! It is very stressful!" said Lance. "I thought you were dying! Or were going to explode! Or something else very, very bad!" He glared at his sister in her dragon form.

"Well, none of those things happened," said Zoe. "What happened is I turned into a dragon!"

"That is not a good thing! Especially because we are about to fight some sort of giant mysterious flying creature and we do not have time to deal with the fact that you are now a dragon!" said Lance, trying and failing to hold back his frustration.

"The fact that I am now a dragon is *extra* useful, then! Now we have five dragons instead of four!" Zoe stuck her dragon tongue out at him.

"Zoe," Lance said very slowly. "Did you know you were going to turn into a dragon?" His mind was spinning. How had she done it? Could she do it again? Could they all do it?

"No," she admitted. "But this is way cooler than what I thought was going to happen."

"What did you think was going to happen when you drank an entire vial of golden elixir?" Lance cried.

Dragon Zoe shrugged, and it was such a Zoe

movement, it made Lance's chest hurt. He knew this was still his sister, but it was strange, seeing her as a dragon.

"I don't know. I thought maybe I would have an army of Zoe replicas! I've only been able to replicate myself like ten times before. Everyone else had done something cool with golden elixir—it was my turn to be awesome. I want to be able to help!"

"You already *are* awesome! You can replicate yourself! You are the youngest recruit ever invited to Camp Claw!" spluttered Lance. He was still in disbelief he was talking to his sister.

Smoke curled out of Zoe's nostrils. "Don't be angry! I didn't do it on purpose! I told you—I was trying to be helpful!"

Lance turned to Infinity. "Infinity, do you think it will wear off? The way my invincibility did when we were battling the Swarm?"

"It was safer for you because of our bond," said Infinity. "I have never seen a human turn into a dragon. I did not even know it was possible."

"But she won't be stuck like this forever, right?" Lance's voice cracked.

Dragon Zoe's eyes widened in her new dragon face. "What if I am?"

Lance knew he had to be brave for Zoe. "You'll always be my sister, no matter what," Lance promised. "Even if you are in dragon form."

"There are tales of shape-shifters, but they are from long ago," Jaws mused. "Dragons used to be able to transform into all kinds of creatures. But I do not remember ever hearing of humans who could turn into dragons."

Bea gasped and held up her hand as if she were waiting to be called on by a teacher.

"Bea, you don't have to raise your hand," said Lance, rubbing his temples.

"This is a very tense conversation. I didn't want to interrupt," she said. "But, Infinity, you can change colors! Isn't that a kind of transformation?"

"Only a very superficial one. It is like dragons who can change size at will. They are manipulating who they are, not completely transforming into something else," Infinity explained.

"Our heart-bond is still strong," said Violet, darting around Zoe. "Zoe, can you hear me in your head?"

Zoe nodded.

"And I you." Violet nuzzled Zoe's face. "I can tell you are nervous. Everything will be all right."

"Will it?" said Arthur, sounding unconvinced. "Zoe is a dragon. Basically a baby dragon."

"Arthur is right! I don't know how to do anything! I can barely breathe fire, and I don't even know if I can fly!" She looked at Violet. "Can I fly?"

"All dragons are born knowing how to fly. So you must know, somehow. But you are not a baby dragon. Not exactly. You are ten in human years, which makes you very young for a dragon, of course, but older than Infinity," Violet explained.

"She's smaller than me, though," said Infinity.

Bea laughed. "Infinity, you sound way too happy about that!"

"It is nice not to be the smallest dragon for once," Infinity admitted.

"So I *am* stronger as a dragon," said Zoe, sounding ridiculously pleased with herself.

Lance let out a groan. "Zoe, this is *not* a good thing! What do we do if we need your replicator skill?"

Zoe tilted her head to the side. "Do you think I can replicate as a dragon?"

"Do not try it," said Neon quickly. "The results could be disastrous." Then he assessed Zoe. "This is very peculiar indeed. Out of curiosity, what exactly were you thinking the moment you drank golden elixir? As we said, it is very unpredictable—even Infinity does not know what will happen when she uses it—but I wonder if your thoughts influenced the result."

"I was thinking that I hoped I could drink it before Lance took it away from me, and then . . ." Zoe gasped. "Then I was thinking about how much faster and agile dragons are than humans! And that if I were a dragon, Lance would never catch me!"

"Should we all drink lots of golden elixir and think about dragons and see what happens?" said Bea. "For science, of course."

"Absolutely not," rumbled Neon. Bea pouted in response. "Anything could have happened to Zoe. She is lucky to be alive. Golden elixir is one of our most powerful gifts, but too much is deadly. I do not know how many times I must tell this to you all."

"Speaking of deadly...," said Arthur in a strained voice. He was staring out of the window at the top of the Dragon Force Tower. "Those things look as if they might end us all, dragon or human."

Flying Krakens

Hurtling toward Dragon's Claw were what appeared to be three giant flying octopuses. Their bodies were splayed like parachutes, and their long tentacles waved in the wind. Their mouths were wide and open, and they were shrieking as they careered through the sky.

"Flying krakens," muttered Violet. "Never a welcome sight."

"You've seen these things before?" spluttered Lance. They looked like nightmares come to life.

"Only once in Dracordia. They arrived out of nowhere, like these ones, and attacked a clan of blue fire dragons who were nesting and trying to protect their eggs. The blue fire dragons called for help, and dozens of other dragons came to their aid. Including me."

"Aw, Violet!" cooed Zoe. "You went to protect the eggs?"

"Dragon eggs are precious," said Violet. "And even though, until recently, I spent most of my life as a solitary dragon, without a clan or a heart-bond, when I hear a dragon cry for help, I go. It is the dragon way."

"So it is," said Jaws. "Tell us, Violet, what happened with the flying krakens?"

"We outnumbered them, but they were vicious. They have eyes all the way around their heads." Violet shook her own head in distaste. "They are impossible to sneak up on."

"Why are they screaming?" said Bea, wincing as the sound grew louder. The flying krakens were getting closer with every moment. Lance knew they didn't have much time.

"That is their battle cry," said Violet. She paused. "Do not be fooled by the fact there are more of us. Flying krakens can divide and multiply in the air."

"Like how I replicate?" said Zoe.

"Or how you *used* to replicate," said Lance, who was still reeling from the fact that his sister was currently stuck in dragon form.

"Not exactly. They are multiplying—and creating new versions of themselves that need to be destroyed. Worst of all, when a flying kraken is struck, it will split and become two or more. And so striking a kraken does not harm it—it only makes matters worse."

"How do you defeat them, then?" Lance burst out.

"It is not easy, as they have few weaknesses," said Violet. "They were immune to my mist, much to my disappointment. But we were lucky that one of the dragons in the battle had ice powers, and we were able to freeze and capture them."

"But none of us have ice powers," said Bea.

"Maybe I do!" said Zoe. "Should I try?"

"NO!" everyone cried at once.

Zoe sighed dramatically, so much that she nearly scorched the edge of one of Jaws's feathered wings.

"Careful!" growled Jaws.

"Sorry! Sorry! Still learning!" Zoe said, and her tail curled beneath her.

Lance's brain could not comprehend that his sister now had a tail. That his sister was a *dragon*.

"This is why you should not try to create ice," grumbled Neon. "Or do anything you have not learned properly. We do not have time for an untrained dragon to try to test themselves! We must be at our best to battle the flying krakens."

"Should we hide from them instead of battling them?" Bea suggested.

"Dragons do not hide," said Jaws, sounding deeply offended.

"Well, not all of us are dragons," said Bea. "At least not yet!" A mischievous smile spread across her face.

"Nobody else is turning into a dragon!" roared Neon. "Those flying krakens will be upon us soon."

"And even if we wanted to hide, they would seek us," said Violet. "They can sense the heartbeats of living things."

Lance took a deep breath. "How do they attack?" he said. "I know they can divide and multiply, but what else?"

"They can shoot power bolts, much like lightning, out of their tentacles," said Violet.

Arthur muttered something under his breath that sounded like a curse word. "Of course they can."

Lance knew they needed a plan, and fast. There was another screeching laugh, and when he looked out the window, he saw that the flying krakens were already beginning to divide and multiply. Where there had been three giant ones, there were now seven. Two had split into three, and one had stayed enormous. As he watched them, he saw the large one continue to grow. It was a horrifying sight, and Lance felt a little bit nauseous at the thought of having to battle these monstrous creatures close-up.

"Are you sure they won't just explode on impact when they land?" said Arthur.

"They may look as if they are falling, but they are flying," said Violet.

"And ice worked last time?" Lance said, walking to the other side of the Dragon Force Tower and locking his eyes on something in the distance.

"Yes! But we do not have ice at our disposal," snapped Violet. "And if we do not want the Dragon Force Tower to be zapped by these things, then we must find another way to battle them!"

"We *do* have ice, though," said Lance, turning to face the others with a wide grin. "We have an entire glacier."

The Glacier was the claw nearest to the Dragon Force Tower, at the edge of Dragon's Claw. Lance pointed out the window toward its windswept white peaks. "We tempt the flying krakens to the Glacier."

Arthur snorted. "And then what? Hope they voluntarily land in a snowdrift and freeze themselves?"

"Not exactly," said Lance. He turned to his dragon. "Infinity, you have a special connection with the Claw, right?"

Infinity nodded. "I do . . ."

"And your connection is so strong that you can even move and reshape the ground with your powers—like when you were able to seal the Volcano's opening."

Infinity reflected for a moment. "I believe it is because I was born here, but also because Dragon's Claw and I both have golden elixir coursing through us. As you know, when the realms collapsed, the last remaining golden elixir from the In-Between formed Dragon's Claw."

"Nobody is allowed to drink any more golden

elixir," interrupted Neon. "We will fight these krakens face-to-face if we need to, but we cannot risk the consequences of taking more golden elixir!"

"Don't worry—we have plenty of golden elixir in our suits," said Lance, stretching in his and reveling in the feeling of power flickering through it. He pointed back at the Glacier. "Do you see that large arch made of ice? If we can get the krakens under there, I can use my erhu to put them in a trance, and Infinity can trap them by bringing down the top of the arch."

"Violet? You have the most experience with the flying krakens," said Jaws. "Do you think it would work?"

Violet's tail twitched back and forth. "I think it is a good idea, but everything has to go to plan for it to be successful. Infinity, do you think you can bring the arch down on command?"

They all turned to Infinity. "I will try," said the dragon quietly.

"And if it doesn't work? What happens then?" asked Arthur. "We get zapped to death by giant flying octopuses?"

"It will work," said Lance. He put his hand on Infinity. "I know you can do this." He nodded, resolute. "Together, we can do this."

"And what should the rest of us do?" said Bea.

Lance grinned. "You lot get to be the bait."

"I bet I could fly faster than a flying kraken," said Zoe as she inspected her butterfly wings and flapped them tentatively.

Lance shook his head. "Zoe, you need to stay here in the tower, where it's safe."

"But you might need me!"

"You've literally just turned into a dragon. Your body is probably still processing all that golden elixir you took. I mean, who knows, I wouldn't be surprised if you turned into a goose mid-battle."

"There's no way I'm turning into a goose," Zoe huffed, clearly offended.

"We don't have time to argue about geese," said Neon. "Lance is right. Zoe, you stay here. And you can be our lookout in case anything else tries to attack us."

Zoe crossed her dragon arms and snorted out a puff of smoke, but she nodded.

Lance could see that the flying krakens were closer now, almost in striking distance, and they were dividing and multiplying faster as they came.

"We need to act now," Lance said, his voice commanding. "Neon, Bea, Arthur, Jaws, and Violet, you all go under the arch in the Glacier and make as much noise and as much of a spectacle as you can. Infinity and I will hide nearby. Do what you can to lure the krakens under the arch, and I will snare them with my music. But make sure you get out from under the arch as quickly as possible so Infinity can bring it down on top of them."

The group nodded and flew off to the Glacier without another word while Zoe stayed behind and kept watch. "Good luck," she called out, her dragon arms still crossed.

The krakens' screeches of laughter were getting louder and more alarming the closer they came. They were varying shades of silver and blue, and they were close enough now that Lance could see the electricity crackling from the ends of their tentacles.

Lance drew a steadying breath, hoping his plan would work. He and Infinity were crouching behind a snowdrift right next to the arch. "Camouflage on," he said, and he was pleased to see that his super-suit instantly changed colors to match the snow around him. He held his hand up and could only barely make out its outline. "Bea, you're a genius," he said under his breath. Next to him, Infinity had used her color-shifting skills to blend in with the snow, so just her eyes and the four jewels at the base of her horns glowed.

"We're over here, you filthy beasts!" Arthur yelled, from under the arch. He and Bea were on their dragons, waving and calling out to the oncoming krakens.

"You flying fools are heading right where we want you!" yelled Bea, who was sitting between Neon's horns.

Lance let out a sigh of relief. The plan was working. The krakens were flying directly toward the arch.

Neon flapped his wings, alternating one after the other, shooting bolts of flashing green electricity with each wingbeat. His electric bolts flew straight at the krakens' lightning strikes, exploding as they crashed together to parry their attacks.

"Careful not to hit the krakens, or they might multiply even more," said Violet.

Neon puffed out his chest. "My aim is immaculate." Neon looked as if he was barely trying as he expertly knocked the onslaught of electricity out of the sky with bolts of his own. Lance took a deep breath and hoped that his song would come as naturally. It was almost time for him to act, and he stepped out from behind the snowdrift, waiting for his moment.

"Retreat," cried Neon as the krakens swooped down to enter the arch. "Retreat!"

Violet, Jaws, and Arthur flew out from the other side of the arch, and Neon reversed as he continued to parry the attacks. "Now, Lance!" he yelled as he turned and flew out from the other side of the arch as well.

The plan was working! The krakens took the bait and swooped under the arch after Neon and the others.

Lance struck his bow on his erhu's strings and played an irresistible song. A melody so sweet, no creature could have resisted. He weaved the notes together like a net, snaring the krakens within it.

You're doing it, Lance! The krakens are stuck under the arch! Infinity said through their bond.

Trap them now! Lance replied. *Bring the top of the arch down. I don't know how long I can hold them.*

Through his bond, Lance could sense Infinity's focus and her strain. The arch above the song-snared krakens began to tremble. As the krakens realized they were trapped, they began to screech in anger. And then, with a ground-shaking *pop*, the arch's roof snapped at both ends and fell on the krakens below.

As the roof fell, the largest flying kraken seemed to shake its way out of the trance. Just before the roof crashed to the ground capturing the rest of the krakens, the biggest one slipped free.

It let out a terrifying screech and launched itself at Lance.

Lance panicked, and without thinking, he flung his erhu at the kraken. It hit the beast with a sickening *thump*, but instead of knocking it back, the erhu split the kraken in two. Each half vibrated violently like a ringing gong and then they each morphed into a fully formed kraken that was just as big as the one Lance had struck.

"Catch it with your song!" cried Infinity.

Lance caught his erhu as it boomeranged back to him, and he played the song again.

The two krakens charged at Lance, their electric tentacles reaching for him like claws.

"It's not working!" Lance yelled, but he continued to play.

Just before the krakens reached Lance, a flash of black and silver shot through the two beasts. Lance followed the flash and saw Jaws shaking the two krakens between his teeth. Once again, the krakens split and started to vibrate.

"You saved me, Jaws," said Lance.

"Technically, it was me and Jaws," said Arthur from Jaws's back.

Lance looked back to the split krakens and gasped. Instead of doubling, the two krakens were now eight.

"We need to find a way to trap them without attacking them," said Bea, as Neon parried an oncoming bolt of lightning.

As if they understood, the krakens stopped firing electricity from their tentacles and rocketed toward the children and the dragons. They knew now that their lightning strikes would be blocked by Neon, but their direct attacks could not be stopped without them multiplying.

Infinity swooped under Lance, pulling him away from an oncoming kraken as Violet, Jaws, and Neon shot out blasts of fire. The blasts stopped the raging krakens in their tracks, but once again they multiplied, and now there were too many for Lance to count.

"We need to think of something else," said Bea. "We can't keep letting them multiply or they'll smother us in numbers."

Lance racked his brain, but he couldn't think of anything other than running away. As he looked around for an escape route, he realized with horror that they were surrounded.

The horde of krakens started firing electricity at the group from every direction. Neon beat his wings, firing back, but there were too many to stop. Bolts of electricity rained down past Neon's defenses. Lance dodged left and right on Infinity's back, but it was only a matter of time before they would be struck.

Just then Lance heard an ear-splitting roar. As he

turned his head toward the sound, a tsunami of wind and purple ice struck them full-on. Infinity's wings folded like a napkin in the blast, and she and Lance tumbled through the air, slamming into the earth.

It took Lance a moment to regain his senses. When Lance looked up, the ground around him was covered in shards of purple ice. His group had been grounded by the blast. And to his great relief, all of the krakens lay motionless on the floor, shards of purple ice piercing their bodies like needles in a pincushion.

Lance looked up to where the blast had come from. A purple dragon was fluttering haphazardly toward them, zigzagging downward before landing clumsily. "Lance, are you okay?" she asked, squeezing him tight in her paws.

It was Zoe.

She had saved them.

16

The Mirage

"Zoe!" Lance said, squeezing dragon Zoe back in a tight hug.

Lance felt another person wrap their arms around them. "That was *incredible*," Bea said, beaming.

Even Arthur came over and joined in the group hug. "Thanks for saving us, Zoe."

"See!" exclaimed Zoe, "I told you golden elixir was a good idea!" She leaped in the air, unable to contain her excitement, throwing all of her friends to the ground.

"Oops," she said. "Sorry . . . I'm still trying to work out my own strength."

"What you did was extraordinary," said Neon. "But you should not have taken that elixir."

"Neon, be nice," said Bea, getting back to her feet. "Zoe just saved us all! We'd be kraken dinner right now if it wasn't for her." Bea turned to her purple dragon friend. "What did you even do? One second I thought we were all going to be electrocuted by flying krakens, and the next, we're being knocked to the ground by a purple ice storm."

Zoe grinned so wide all of her dragon teeth glistened in the sun. "I don't really know how I did it. I saw all of you were in danger, so I flew over as fast as I could, and I was so determined to save you, I just roared as loudly as possible and a gigantic wave of ice came out."

"It was one of the coolest things I've ever seen," said Arthur. "So smart to use ice shards that were sharp enough to take out the krakens but wouldn't hurt us."

"I do not think that was on purpose," said Neon, mostly to himself.

"Of course it was!" said Lance, turning to his sister. "You were amazing. I'm sorry I doubted you."

Zoe shrugged. "I understand. It probably wasn't a good idea to take all that golden elixir, and I know I'm lucky to be okay. But hey, we're all still here and

I'm still me. Just . . . dragon me! And most important, we still have a world to save."

Zoe was the luckiest person that Lance knew. He admired how bold and carefree and determined she was, and it had always served her well. He hoped that her luck would rub off on all of them. Lance smiled back at his sister.

"What's next?" he asked the group.

"Before those krakens showed up, we were trying to agree how to defeat the Petrifiers. If we believe what the Swarm said, we have to find a way to reflect a Petrifiers' attack back on itself," said Bea, adjusting her glasses.

Infinity gazed at them all. "I can feel the Devourer growing closer. We are running out of time. I think Lance is right. The Mirage is our best shot to get something that will help us fight the Petrifiers and the Devourer."

She paused, then added, "There is something I didn't tell you earlier. After I had succeeded in passing the Mirage's challenge, the Mirage revealed that everyone who enters its domain for the first time is offered a challenge. Anyone who refuses is automatically lost for all eternity in the Mirage. Those who accept must then complete an extraordinary challenge. If they succeed, they are rewarded. If they are unsuccessful, they are lost forever." Infinity paused again, letting the group process what she had just said.

"We were lucky to have survived the krakens," said Neon. "We were not prepared. We should not make the same mistake with the Petrifiers. I think that we should all go into the Mirage, accept its challenge, and ask that it help us face the Petrifiers and the Devourer if we succeed."

"I'm in!" said Zoe, without a second's thought.

Lance glared affectionately at his dragon sister. "I'm in too."

Bea nodded. "Me too."

The dragons all nodded in assent.

"So let me get this straight," Arthur said with a frown. "The plan is to go into the Mirage, which is *so* dangerous that even the Dragon Force avoid it, and then ask the Mirage if it would be so kind as to help us power up to defeat the Petrifiers if we are able to overcome whatever outrageous challenge the Mirage gives us?"

Neon nodded. "Precisely."

Arthur's frown deepened. "I know I said this before, but aren't we just putting ourselves in unnecessary danger?"

"The world is ending," said Neon, his voice solemn. "We have never been in more danger."

Bea gave Neon a nudge. "Your motivational skills need work."

Lance took a step forward and addressed the group. "Look, I think what Neon is trying to say is that we can't just charge into the Devourer's den and expect to defeat the Devourer and all of his Petrifiers. We only have one shot at saving the Dragon Force, so we need to prepare as much as we can. We're doomed if we think we can just fly into an army of Petrifiers and save the day. We need to find a way to attack their weaknesses."

"Maybe," said Arthur, crossing his arms.

"I know you're afraid of what might happen in the Mirage. I am too. But that's a good thing. We'll be facing our fears together, and that will prepare us even better for the Petrifiers. It's like training a muscle. The more you work it, the stronger it gets.

And so the more we work to conquer our fears, the stronger we'll be against the Petrifiers."

Jaws nodded and turned to Arthur. "I think Lance may be right."

"You remember how hard it was to face one Petrifier," Lance continued. "There is a whole army of them in the den. If we can't overcome our fears in the Mirage, we won't stand a chance against the Petrifiers and the Devourer."

Arthur let out a breath. "Okay, okay. I get it. But if one of us gets lost forever in the Mirage, don't say this was my idea."

Lance walked over to Arthur and put a hand on each of his shoulders. He looked him straight in the eyes. "We're a team. No one gets left behind. Not you. Not me. None of us. We are going to go in and face our fears together. We all look out for one another."

Bea walked over and put her hand on Arthur's left shoulder, and Zoe fluttered over and put her paw on his right.

"We can do this," Bea said.

"Together we're unstoppable," said Zoe.

Arthur looked at his friends for a long moment, his eyes round with gratitude. Then he uncrossed his arms and wrapped them around Bea, Zoe, and Lance in a group hug.

Lance wasn't sure if Arthur had ever had friends he really trusted, and he was happy they could show him that things could be different. That he could be part of a team. "You're not getting rid of any of us, Arthur."

Arthur squeezed the group in his arms, holding them tight for a few moments before letting go. He cleared his throat. "So, what are we waiting for? Let's go into the Mirage."

The dragons and their riders flew to the edge of the Glacier, which bordered the swirling clouds of the Mirage. In the distance, Lance could see the Wild Wood on the other side of the Mirage. It was overgrown with trees and plants and vegetation, and Lance knew it was where the dragons liked to train and where powers could be awakened because of the magic flowing from the trees to the land and back again. It was, after all, where Bea and Arthur had discovered their powers.

From his time at Camp Claw, Lance knew there was dragon magic, and powers that could be awakened, but also that the magic of nature was just as potent. If they ever did defeat the Devourer, and he ever went back to his home in New London, near his own woods, he would never take any of it for granted, ever. He would appreciate every tree and blossom he saw.

He glanced over at his sister in her dragon form and hoped that when he did go home, Zoe would be with him, and she would be herself. He'd never take his sister for granted again, either.

But he did have to admit that Zoe seemed quite happy being a dragon. She appeared to be turning into a stronger flier with every passing moment.

"What was it like in there?" Bea asked, breaking the silence as the group all stared into the Mirage's swirling clouds.

"Everyone will experience the Mirage differently," said Infinity. "Even now, looking in, we will see different things."

Lance had flown over the Mirage a few times before, and he recalled that it did look different on each occasion. Now it was a swirling dark-green cloud cut with slick black streaks that appeared like eels. "What does it look like to you, Zoe?"

She tilted her head as she peered in. "It looks like a purple swirl, similar to water spinning down a drain." She stared a moment longer into the Mirage before turning to Infinity. "What challenge did the Mirage give you?" Zoe asked. "Maybe we'll have to do something similar."

"My challenge was to simply get out," said Infinity. "As I was only a hatchling, my wings were new and weak. I was thrown into a storm so strong and violent that I thought the wind might tear my wings off. But I persevered and found my way out."

Lance saw Zoe shudder, and he was glad that she wasn't going alone into the Mirage. He'd be there to protect her.

"Now the Mirage is calm and peaceful for me every time I return," Infinity continued. "As for our challenge, my guess will be as good as yours. But know that the Mirage is a place where nothing is as it seems. Don't lose hope."

"Is everyone ready?" Neon asked.

The group nodded, everyone's expressions solemn as they prepared themselves mentally for the Mirage.

Lance tightened his grip around Infinity's neck and the group dived into the mist.

Flying through the Mirage felt exactly as it looked—like flying through a green cloud full of floating eels. Lance dodged left and right as they flew, trying to avoid floating pests.

Why are you zigzagging through the air? Infinity asked through their bond.

To avoid all of these gross floating eels. Don't you see them?

Nothing is as it seems in the Mirage, Infinity replied.

"Whoa!" yelled Zoe, zooming past them. "Unicorns! Rainbows and waterfalls! This place is *awesome*!"

Lance shot through the mist after his sister. "Focus, Zoe!"

"I am focused! This place is *amazing*!"

Before Lance could reply, there was a lightning strike through the air.

The group huddled together, their backs to each other in a protective stance.

"Did everyone see that?" Lance asked.

"I saw it," said Zoe.

"Me too," said Bea.

"A group of visitors," said a voice that sounded as if the wind was whispering in Lance's ear. The closeness of it made Lance uneasy. "What a treat for me. I have not had a new human or dragon visitor in a very, very long time. Infinity, is it you who has brought me new challengers? Have you grown bored of exploring my depths on your own?"

"We've come to make a deal with you," said Infinity.

"How wonderful," the voice replied. "Making deals is the delight of my existence. Or what can be considered an existence."

"The New World is in grave danger," Infinity replied. "A great devourer is coming, and he uses fear to petrify his prey."

"I know the Devourer you speak of. Do you not think I know what happens on the Claw? The Devourer's minions—I believe you refer to them as Petrifiers—have put such fear in the Dragon Force that they have been petrified, frozen for eternity, or at least until they are . . . devoured."

"We are going to defeat the Devourer and his Petrifiers and save the Dragon Force," said Infinity defiantly. "No one is going to be devoured."

"Tell me why you have you come," the voice demanded.

"To defeat the Petrifiers and the Devourer, we know we must reflect their attacks back onto themselves, to make them see their own fears. You are the master of matters of the mind, and if you are able to grant us the ability to reflect a person's fear back onto themselves, then we will do any challenge you present," said Lance with as much confidence as he could muster.

"Of course that is within my power," the voice boasted. "But this is a dangerous request. Are you certain?"

Infinity looked around at the group, and there was a collective nod.

"Very well," the voice replied.

The fog swirled around them, tendrils of smoke licking their super-suits. One of the tendrils of smoke wrapped around Lance's waist and pulled him through the sky. Lance had never traveled so fast before—it felt faster than the speed of light. So fast that the smoke and colors around him couldn't keep up. The colors started to fall behind, replaced by white, like water dripping down a window pane. Faster and faster he flew through the air, until the color faded away completely and everything was white. A white void. When he came to a halt, the tendril of smoke had disappeared, and Lance found he was standing on a solid white floor. He looked around, but everything was so white that he couldn't tell where the floor ended and where the air started. It was eerily quiet.

"Hello?" Lance called out. The air seemed to soak up his words as soon as they left his mouth, as if he were yelling into a pillow.

"Hello!" he called out again, louder this time. But what came out was barely a whisper.

Two large red eyes appeared in the white space in front of him, and despite himself, a thread of fear curled its way through him.

The eyes floated closer, getting larger as they approached. They were perfectly circular, red eyes with a black vertical slit through the center.

The eyes floated steadily closer until Lance could nearly reach out and touch them. He realized it was some sort of snake.

"Hello, Lance," the snake whispered, its forked tongue flicking out of its mouth.

"Where am I?" Lance mumbled, trying to squash his fear. *It isn't real. It isn't real*, he told himself.

"Not important," the snake replied. "The important question is: Where do you want to be? Or perhaps an even better question is . . . where *don't* you want to be?"

"You're not real!" Lance said, puffing his chest out slightly and pushing the thread of fear out of his body. "I'm not afraid of you."

"What are you afraid of then, Lance?"

Each eye began to swirl like a spinning top, and three enormous tigers crawled out of pockets in the white void around Lance.

"Perhaps tigers are your weakness?" the voice continued.

"I'm not afraid," said Lance, as he wielded his erhu in front of him.

As the tigers circled Lance, he saw that they were at least twice the size of normal tigers. One of the animals hissed and bared its huge teeth at Lance, and he saw they glinted like shards of glass.

"How about now?" said the voice of the Mirage.

"I'm not afraid," Lance repeated, willing himself to believe the words.

"Not yet," said the voice. There was a lightning strike that cut through the sky, and when it was gone, it took all the light with it, plunging Lance and the three tigers into darkness.

Lance pulled his super-suit's helmet on and was relieved when he could see the three tigers with his suit's night vision.

"Impressive suit," the voice said. "But your challenge has just begun."

Lance could see that the tigers were still circling him, hissing and baring their teeth as they did. And then, without warning, they pounced.

Lance jumped straight up into the air, and the tigers crashed into each other.

The closest tiger roared and lunged up at Lance, who was still floating above them.

Lance held his ground and swung his erhu at the beast, but the tiger exploded into a cloud of smoke and reappeared behind him. Lance landed gracefully on the ground.

The two other tigers let out a roar and leaped at Lance from both sides. Lance swung his erhu again in a circle, but once again the tigers disappeared as Lance struck them, leaving a cloud of smoke and reappearing on the other side of him.

The tigers continued lunging at Lance, getting faster and more aggressive with each attack. Lance felt lucky to have his super-suit. He swung in all directions, keeping the tigers at a distance. With lunge after lunge, Lance parried the tigers away. But they were relentless and ever faster, and Lance was running out of breath. He was getting tired.

I can't go on like this forever, Lance thought. *There has to be a way to defeat these things.* He dashed away from the tigers, breaking the cycle of lunging and swinging, and the tigers chased after him. It was no use—even with the super-suit, the tigers were faster, and they were gaining on him. As he looked back, their teeth caught his eye—they glistened unnaturally. *Maybe the secret is in their teeth*, he thought. Lance strapped his erhu back behind him and turned to face the three tigers. The one in front lunged, and Lance caught its jaws with his bare hands. He struggled against the tiger, holding its jaws away from his head, and then, with a mighty tug, Lance ripped its teeth out of its skull and the tiger disappeared with a *poof*, leaving only a cloud of smoke, but this time, the tiger didn't reappear.

Lance pumped his fist in the air. "Yes!"

A second tiger lunged at Lance, and this time, Lance twisted his body as he caught its jaws, like a bullfighter waving their red flag. Lance pulled its jaws out as he turned and the tiger disappeared in smoke.

The last tiger stopped and stared at Lance before turning and leaping away, disappearing into a cloud of smoke before it hit the ground.

Lance let out a sigh of relief and caught his breath.

"You've done well, Lance," said the voice, the red eyes appearing in front of him again. "Clearly, you are a brave soul. Your challenge is complete. I will bring you back now. And I am surprised to say that only one of your group did not succeed."

Lance felt a pit form in his stomach. "What do you mean?"

"You are an exceedingly impressive group. I did not expect more than one or at most two of you to make it past my challenges. But I was wrong. All of you have made it out except one."

"Who didn't pass the challenge?" Lance asked, but in his heart he knew.

"Your sister, of course. Brave, but foolhardy."

"Can she still make it out?" Lance said, trying to hold back tears.

"See for yourself," the voice replied.

Zoe appeared in the white void as if emerging from behind a waterfall. She was still in dragon form and hanging upside down from her tail, a ring of smoke holding her in the air. Her body was limp and she looked unconscious, but Lance could see her eyes darting around beneath her eyelids.

Lance leaped toward his sister, his super-suit propelling him through the air. "Zoe!"

He flew toward Zoe, but the ground between them expanded, and no matter how fast he ran or jumped, Zoe kept getting farther away.

"Lance, is that you?" Zoe replied, but her eyes were still closed.

"Yes! Zoe, it's me! Wake up!" Lance removed his helmet. "You need to wake up!"

Zoe shook her head and smiled. "Lance...stop...teasing," she said, her words coming out slow and choppy. "It's bedtime. It's time to go to sleep. We've got school tomorrow."

"Zoe, you need to wake up! Open your eyes! You're in the Mirage—you aren't at home. Zoe, wake up!"

Lance yelled as loudly as he could, but his sister didn't respond anymore. She was breathing deeper now.

"She is lost in her own mind," said the voice. "She belongs to me now."

Lance went numb. "Let her go!" he cried, and he hurled his erhu at the red eyes above him. The erhu passed through them with little effect and returned to Lance's outstretched hand.

"I like your spirit, Lance, and I am feeling generous today."

As the voice spoke, the white void around him began to swirl, and shades of green, blue, and yellow appeared around him.

Bang!

The ground shook, and the swirling colors snapped into place. Lance found himself in a large meadow with blue skies overhead. Zoe was still dangling upside down on the other side of the meadow.

"If you can get to your sister, I'll set her free."

The ground beneath Lance fell away until he was left swaying on a rope above a bottomless pit.

Lance steadied himself and ran down the rope toward his sister, his super-suit giving him balance. Lance leaped through the air and hit the ground running. He was halfway to his sister now and he had a clear path to her.

I'm going to save Zoe, Lance told himself. *I'm not leaving her behind.*

Lance was a stone's throw away when a wall of ice shot out of the ground. It went impossibly high and was as wide as his eyes could see. Lance grabbed his erhu and held it out in front of him like a battering ram. He leaped straight at the wall and was surprised to find that he smashed right through it.

He was not expecting to see what lay in front of him.

The other side of the wall was a raging blizzard. Wind howled in his ears, and frost nipped at his cheeks. He pulled his helmet over his head, shielding himself from the harsh conditions. He could still make out Zoe, but he was farther from her now than when he'd started. He sprinted toward her, determined to save her.

But with each step he took, the ground between them stretched and expanded, sending Zoe farther and farther into the tundra. Another ice wall shot up in front of Lance, and he swung his erhu at it with all his might. The wall shattered, but to Lance's shock, so did his erhu. The end of his instrument splintered into a thousand pieces, leaving only the handle.

"No!" Lance cried.

He threw his erhu to the ground and sprinted forward, determined to get to Zoe. But as he ran, his legs began to feel heavy. The ground beneath him softened, and he started to sink into the ground. He found that he was running in waist-deep snow. His legs and lungs were burning, but he pushed through the pain.

As he pushed, Lance felt the hairs on the back of his neck stand up, and then there was a flash of lightning from the sky. The bolt struck him in the chest, and Lance fell on his hands and knees. Everything went black for a moment. When Lance opened his eyes, the wind was screaming in his ears again and he could feel the sting of the frost and ice on his skin. He looked down and saw that the lightning bolt had somehow removed his super-suit, and he was back in the clothes he wore when he'd first arrived at Camp Claw. Lance crossed his arms over his chest and continued to push through the blizzard. He looked up and gasped. Zoe was so far away now he could barely see her.

Lance fell to his knees and sobbed. And for the first time since he had entered the Mirage, he felt fear. It clenched his heart like a fist.

He lay there, sobbing, feeling the failure wash over him.

"Take me," Lance said.

"Pardon?" the voice replied.

"Take me instead. Let my sister go."

"What would I want with you?"

"I'll give you anything," said Lance between sobs. "Just let Zoe go."

"Give me your memories. Give me your bravery

and your music and your heart. Give me what makes *you* you. After all, one cannot truly take these things if they are not willingly given."

Lance closed his eyes. "Okay."

In his mind's eye, Lance saw himself and his sister spotting their first dragon on their walk home from school through the woods. It was a small red dragon that looked a bit like a large rooster. He laughed as he pointed it out to his sister. And then the memory disappeared like petals in the wind. Another memory of his sister appeared. This time they were having dinner with their parents at home, eating homemade noodles.

"No!" Lance cried. "I take it back! Give me back my memories!"

"The deal is done."

Fear gripped Lance like a vice. He couldn't move. He couldn't breathe. He felt as if his whole body was frozen. He couldn't believe that he was never going to see his sister or his parents or anyone else ever again.

This can't be happening, he told himself. *This can't be happening.*

And then the realization came to Lance. *This isn't happening*, he told himself. *This isn't real. This isn't happening.* "This isn't real! This isn't happening!" he cried.

Lance felt a ball of warmth in his chest. The feeling in his fingers started trickling back. He looked down at his hands and saw that his super-suit was reappearing. "*This isn't happening*," he repeated. "None of this is real."

He reached for his erhu strapped to his back. *I know it's here. I know it's here.* He felt his hand close around the smooth wood handle of his erhu, and he wielded it in front of him.

"Let me out!" Lance yelled, and he slashed through the air with his erhu. The air ripped like canvas. Lance leaped through the opening and rolled onto soft, warm grass. When he looked around, he found he was on a small island floating in a clear blue sky.

"Lance, you made it!" yelled a voice. It was Infinity!

Infinity bounded over to him and nuzzled his cheek. Behind her, Lance saw Violet and Jaws hovering in the air, and Arthur was there too, jogging toward him.

"Arthur, you made it!" said Lance.

"Obviously," he said. He tapped his temples with a finger. "My mind is like a steel trap."

"Where are the others?" Lance asked, trying to hide the concern in his voice.

"We are the only ones who have escaped so far," said Infinity. "I escaped first, and Violet, Jaws, and Arthur got out a few moments before you."

A ripping sound tore through the air, and a hole opened in the sky above them. Bea leaped out and landed with a somersault on the ground next to them.

"Bea!" cried Lance, running over and hugging her. "I'm so glad you made it out!"

There was another ripping sound, and Neon appeared in the center of the group, roaring and spitting fire as he emerged.

"Neon, you're free!" Jaws roared. "Be calm!"

"That was deeply, deeply unpleasant," said Neon, shaking his head as if he was trying to clear it.

Bea jumped up on his back and patted his neck. "I'm so glad you made it out."

"Me too," said Neon. He looked around, surveying the group. "Where is Zoe?"

The group was silent.

"She hasn't made it out yet," said Jaws.

Violet exhaled. "She's coming. I am sure of it."

Fear gripped Lance's heart again. What if the Mirage was telling the truth? What if Zoe *had* gotten lost forever and it really had been her helplessly dangling on the other side of the meadow?

Lance felt someone embrace him from behind. His heart leaped. Was it Zoe? He turned and tried not to show the disappointment in his face when he saw it was Arthur and Bea wrapping him in a hug.

"Zoe is one of the strongest people I've ever met," Arthur said, his arm still wrapped around Lance. "She's going to make it."

Lance took a breath and let himself believe the words Arthur was saying. "She's going to make it," he repeated, as if saying them out loud would make them true. "She's going to make it."

"She's going to make it," Bea echoed.

Violet whipped her head toward the left side of the small island. "My heart can sense something coming..."

A loud *crack* whipped through the air.

And then Zoe burst through a rip at the edge of the island, rolling head over heels across the ground before coming to an abrupt stop on her belly at the center of the group, her dragon tongue flopping onto the ground.

"Well, *that* was pretty scary," she said. She gingerly stood up and dusted herself off with her paws.

Lance ran to his sister and wrapped his arms around her dragon belly. Even in her dragon form, she was still *Zoe*, and she was here, she was really here—she had made it. They had all made it. He felt his whole body relax as the truth sank in. They had made it—they had survived the Mirage. "I'm so happy you're okay," he told her.

"I'm happy you're okay too," said Zoe, giving him her dragon grin. She looked around and took stock of the group. "We've all made it! Hooray!" she cried.

A gust of wind rushed past them. "You are an exceptional group of individuals," the voice of the Mirage said. "Every being, human or dragon, has their own way of dealing with fear. Some run, and some look to conquer it. All of you were brave, but you drew strength from different places. Lance with love, caring for others, and a great appreciation for life. Zoe with self-confidence and a thirst for adventure. Bea with hope. A zealousness and passion for progress. Arthur with determination. I sensed grit and also an undertone of an anger there, but your heart is good. As for your dragons, they drew strength in the same way, which is unsurprising as your bonds are among the strongest that I have witnessed. And you are even stronger as a team. I wish you luck in your quest to save the New World. I, of course, will stay true to my word. I will imbue each of your suits or scales with my essence. It will enable you to reflect fears back to those who try to petrify you. But you must master your fears as you have done here for the essence to work."

Wisps of white fog rolled out from the edges of the island and swirled around the group, whipping blades of grass into the air. And then the streams of fog flowed into the chest of each Dragon Force member, the suits and scales soaking in the Mirage's essence, until all the fog was gone and the sky was clear again. Lance looked down at his super-suit and saw that it had a reflective quality to it now, like an extra layer of armor.

"Now be gone," said the voice. Without any more notice, the island shot up into the sky, higher and higher, until Lance saw a thick layer of green fog above. It looked like the surface of the Mirage when they'd first gone in. The island punched through the fog, and the group found themselves back on the Claw. The island came to an abrupt halt, and the group continued to fly up into the air, the dragons swooping under their riders, catching them with ease. When Lance looked back down, the island that had carried them had disappeared, leaving only the Mirage's mysterious swirling fog in sight.

The Legendary Tree

As the group flew back onto the familiar ground of the Palm, they all grinned at one another and whooped with joy.

They had done it. They had all faced their various fears and conquered them. Lance knew now that he truly would do anything to protect his sister and Infinity, and that gave him a strength he had not known he possessed.

"Fears conquered! Suits upgraded! Now, according to the Swarm's intel, all we need are blood-berry seeds," said Bea with her usual optimism. "And then we can save everyone!"

"You make it sound so easy," said Lance with a laugh. He turned to the dragons. "What exactly is a blood berry, anyway?"

"I believe the Swarm was speaking of the berries that grow on a legendary tree dragons know as the blood-berry tree," said Jaws.

"Where is it?" said Lance.

"Nearly all dragons have heard of the blood-berry tree," said Neon.

"And let me guess ... few have seen it?" Lance arched an eyebrow.

"A good guess," said Jaws. "I myself do not even know if it is real or not."

"Since this intel came directly out of the Swarm's brain, I think we can assume it is real," Arthur pointed out. "What makes this tree special?"

"There is only one of its kind. Legend has it that the blood-berry tree does not drink water, but blood that has been spilled on the earth. Its roots are said to be supremely powerful and far-reaching. Every drop of blood that hits the earth is said to flow to this tree as rain flows to the sea."

"Gross," snorted Zoe.

"Perhaps," Neon continued. "But there are others who see this as the greatest wonder in our realm. Some dragons will even spill the blood of a slain loved one as an offering to the blood-berry tree."

Bea put her hands on her hips. "And nobody knows where this blood-sucking tree actually is?"

"I think," said Arthur, "that the all-knowing dragons are saying this is something we have to figure out together."

"Very good, human," said Violet, eyes twinkling. "I have only heard that it is at the far reaches of the Dragon Realm."

"But the Dragon Realm doesn't exist anymore!" Zoe yelled, jets of purple fire shooting out of her nose. She fluttered backward, surprised again by her new dragon abilities.

Arthur waved the smoke away with his hand. "Does that mean the tree might have been lost in the Great Collapse?"

Violet nodded. "That is a possibility. I do not know if the blood-berry tree made it into the New World when the Dragon Realm and the Human Realm collided, and if it did, I do not know where it is."

"Maybe I can try to locate it with my powers," Arthur said, closing his eyes and bringing his fingertips to his temples. "If anyone knows anything else about it, now is the time to tell me. The more I can visualize it, the better chance I have of finding it."

"Supposedly it is one tree that rises up out of the center of an enchanted lake," said Jaws.

"Of course it is an enchanted lake," grumbled Lance. "It couldn't be a normal, nonthreatening lake."

"Of course not," said Bea. "That would be too easy."

Arthur pursed his lips, his eyes still closed. "Shh! Don't distract me. Back to the lake—what kind of enchantment?"

"The legends say the tree takes blood to give life—for every drop of blood it takes, it releases a drop of enchanted water. This water heals and extends the life of those who come into contact with it. And so the lake is called the Lake of Life."

"But the most precious gift of the blood-berry tree is the blood berries themselves. They are meant to have supreme healing properties," said Violet. "I am not surprised that these would be able to unpetrify the petrified."

"Could these blood berries fix me?" said Zoe quietly. "Turn me back into myself?"

Lance reached out and patted his sister on her head. It was still strange that she had scales now, but he knew no matter what form Zoe was in, he would always support her.

"What happened to you is not something that needs healing, but mastering," said Infinity.

The group was quiet for a moment while Arthur continued to search for the tree, his brow furrowed and his hands trembling slightly. "There are so many trees in the New World. I can't make my way through all of them. It's too tiring. I don't know if I can find it before I exhaust myself."

Jaws padded over toward Arthur. "You can do it. I believe in you. I can feel your power growing each time you use it. And I can sense our bond strengthening as we gain each other's trust. You are ready for me to supercharge you through our bond. It may give you the boost you need to locate the tree."

Jaws lowered his head and closed his eyes. As he did, Arthur's hands steadied and the ground began to tremble. Lance saw a bead of sweat drip down Arthur's nose.

"Good. Very good," said Jaws, his voice still low and soothing. "Keep searching."

Arthur scrunched up his face, and his hands began trembling again. Lance could feel Arthur's power growing. Loose pebbles and rocks started floating into the air around Arthur, and the ground beneath him fractured and cracked as if his search for the tree was pulling the earth apart. "Whoa!" said Lance. It was incredible to watch.

Another moment passed before Arthur threw up his arms and sighed. The earth stilled, and the suspended rocks fell back to the ground. "Argh! There are just *too* many trees! I can't do it, Jaws." He hung his head. "I'm sorry. I could feel you supercharging me, but it wasn't enough. There's just too much to search."

Lance placed his hand on Arthur's shoulder. "That was incredible. You did your best. And your bond with Jaws is strong enough that you can supercharge each other now. That is something to be proud of."

Arthur looked up at Lance and gave him half a smile. "Thanks. But my best isn't good enough."

"Arthur, don't be so hard on yourself. We wouldn't have gotten nearly this far without you," said Lance.

"There has to be something we can do," said Bea. "What if Arthur tried to use some more golden elixir? It worked with the Swarm."

Lance balked. "You've got to be kidding, right?" He glanced at Zoe. "No offense, Zoe."

Bea held her hands up. "Sorry. You're right. I know that is probably a terrible idea. I just don't know what other options we have."

"Maybe you could re-create some blood berries with molecule magic?" Lance asked.

Bea signed. "I wish. But I don't know enough about the blood berries to re-create them. And I still need the same raw materials, and it sounds as if the tree takes blood from all over the New World. That would be practically impossible for me to re-create."

"That's it!" Arthur cried, his eyes lighting up.

The group stared at him expectantly.

"If the blood-berry tree is in the New World, any blood that drops to the earth will flow to the tree, right?"

Neon nodded. "Yes . . . that is correct."

Arthur peeled his glove back and held out his hand to Jaws. "Prick my finger."

Jaws hesitated a moment before swiping a claw at

Arthur's outstretched hand, expertly opening a small cut on Arthur's index finger.

"Perfect," said Arthur as he squeezed a drop of blood out and let it fall to the soil. He placed one hand on the earth where his blood fell, and he brought the other hand to his temple, closing his eyes. Arthur flashed a smile. "I think I know how to get to the blood-berry tree." He paused and shook his head. "It's strange. I am sensing it is close, but what's weird is that there isn't a lake there. It's at the bottom of a canyon where it never stops raining."

"I think I know the place you speak of," said Neon. "It's in Dracordia, a few hundred miles away."

"Imagine if we have been right by the legendary blood-berry tree all this time?" said Jaws.

"Let us get going," said Violet.

Arthur leaped up onto Jaws's back. "I'll lead the way."

Violet turned to Zoe. "Climb onto my back and hold on. Those butterfly wings of yours, as pretty as they are, aren't built for speed."

Zoe fluttered onto Violet's back, and the group shot up into the sky.

18

Dracordia

Lance's heart raced in his chest as they flew off the Claw and into Dracordia. Even though their group had already journeyed through Dracordia to defeat the Swarm, this was still the land of the dragons, and it made him both excited and anxious. The dragons of Dracordia were known to be some of the least friendly and most ferocious dragons, with little interest in finding their heart-bonded humans.

Dracordia was like nowhere else Lance had ever seen. There were all kinds of strange creatures, not just dragons. After they had been flying for only a short period, Lance saw what looked like a family of whales hovering midair over a patch of trees. As he looked closer, he saw the creatures were sucking the fruit and leaves off the branches below with such force that it looked as if the trees were caught in a tornado.

What are those whale-looking things? Lance asked Infinity through their bond.

I do not know what they are called. I too have rarely left the Claw, and much of Dracordia is as new to me as it is to you.

Lance liked the thought that he and Infinity were discovering Dracordia and its inhabitants together, and he felt lucky to have their bond. *Let's call them tornado whales.*

Tornado whales it is. Infinity responded with such warmth that Lance knew Infinity felt the same way about him.

As they continued inland, Lance was surprised to find it was raining despite the clear skies and sunshine. He scanned the horizon and saw they were surrounded by the most dazzling rainbows he'd ever seen. The entire sky was technicolor, as if Lance was looking through a kaleidoscope.

"I've never seen a sky more beautiful," said Bea.

"How is it raining when there are no clouds?" Lance asked.

"The rain is said to come from weeping stars," Neon replied, "and it bends the light in different ways from normal water. It is why the sky looks so different here above the canyon."

They had been flying for a few hours when Arthur and Jaws paused. "We're close," said Arthur as he led the group down to the bottom of a vast canyon. The group landed on a flat plain of soil that was riddled with puddles. "It's somewhere here," said Arthur, coming to a halt on Jaws's back and scanning the ground.

Bea scratched her head. "Arthur, are you sure this is the right place? I don't see any trees."

Arthur pointed at a puddle on the ground that was roughly the size of a large pot. "It's here."

"That doesn't look like a tree," said Zoe. "Unless that tiny puddle is actually a puddle-lake, and it's a really small tree in the puddle?"

Arthur shook his head. "Don't be ridiculous. The tree itself isn't here. I think this puddle is actually a portal that will take us to the blood-berry tree. I'm not able to pathfind past this portal, but I know that this is the way to the tree."

"There is no way I'm fitting through that puddle, and I'm the smallest dragon here," huffed Zoe.

"Just trust me," said Arthur. "Who wants to go first? I think we can go in pairs. Dragon and rider."

Zoe snorted a puff of smoke at Arthur.

"Sorry, Zoe. In your case, a dragon-and-dragon pair will work as well," said Arthur.

"I'll go first with Violet!" said Zoe, gliding forward on her heart-bonded dragon.

"I don't think that is a good idea," said Lance. "You've put yourself in enough danger for one day. Let Infinity and me go first."

Before Zoe had a chance to object, Lance pulled his helmet on, and Infinity placed one of her paws in the puddle.

"Ready?" Arthur asked.

Lance and Infinity nodded.

"Close your eyes and think of the blood-berry tree."

Lance closed his eyes as Arthur instructed. He pictured a towering tree ripe with red berries, its trunk thick and tall. And then suddenly Lance was free-falling. The puddle pulled him and Infinity into its waters. There was a flash of light, and Lance found he was swimming through sky-blue water with Infinity. It took Lance a moment to realize that his suit's helmet had activated itself and he could breathe and see clearly underwater.

The water felt *amazing*. It was the most refreshing water he'd ever been in, and it felt as if it was energizing him, like one of Violet's healing mists.

This way to the surface, Infinity said through their bond, shooting them out into the sky.

Lance squinted as his eyes adjusted to the bright sunlight. A moment later his group shot out of the water behind him. First Zoe and Violet, then Bea and Neon, and finally Arthur and Jaws.

"This must be the Lake of Life," said Lance, looking around for an island or any sign of land, but the sky-blue water stretched on as far as he could see in every direction. "Did everyone else feel how amazing the water felt?"

"I've never felt better," said Zoe, doing a backflip in the air.

"This water definitely has some magical properties

to it," said Bea, who was hovering above the lake on Neon and inspecting it carefully with her hands, using her powers to analyze the lake's water.

The water certainly looked special to Lance. As he inspected the water's surface, he saw that it sparkled like the night sky. He wondered whether drinking any of the water would make him stronger or help him live longer, and what the consequences would be. He knew now, from golden elixir, that magic and power were unpredictable.

As if anticipating the question, Neon spoke. "The Lake of Life water is too potent to drink, even for dragons. Even one sip could be fatal, despite being called the Lake of Life. The power in this lake is far too much for any living creature, human or dragon. And the flesh of the berries we seek is even more potent than the water, so be sure not to eat it."

There was a flapping behind them, and Lance whirled in the air to see three unfamiliar dragons hovering above. They were all various shades of green, like leaves come to life. Two were large, even bigger than Neon, and the one in the middle—the one with the darkest green scales—wasn't as big as the others. It was long and slender, like Violet, with long whiskers that streamed out behind it and furry eyebrows.

"How dare you bring humans to the Lake of Life," hissed the middle dragon. "This is a sacred place!"

"How dare you bring humans to Dracordia at all!" added the one on the right who had light-green diamond spikes running down its back. It blew out a threatening puff of warning smoke. "Be gone, and be gone now."

"We do not like to fight other dragons, but dragons who are on the side of humans are barely dragons at all," sneered the third dragon, who had one long horn protruding from its forehead, like a unicorn. "You are traitors to yourself. You allow humans to use you for their own protection. In this New World, dragons do not need humans. Stay in Dracordia. Let it become a new Dragon Realm."

"For one to speak so callously, one must have never known the joy of a human–heart-bond," rumbled Jaws. "Humans and dragons are stronger together."

"Why would I want to make humans stronger?" spat the small green dragon. "We do not need them.

We have powers without them. It is only humans who need us."

"Your ignorance is staggering," said Neon. "Do not embarrass yourself."

Lance had never encountered dragons so openly hostile to humans, and he was glad they had their heart-bonded dragons on their side.

"I used to be like you three," said Violet. "Not understanding why some dragons would debase themselves by allowing a human to ride them."

"I see that you do not have a human rider," said the one with the diamond spikes. "Why do you travel with those who do?"

"Do not be mistaken by what your eyes see," Violet went on. "My heart-bonded human is here."

The three dragons stared at one another and then all inhaled as one.

The dragon with the horn gasped, focusing its attention onto Zoe.

Infinity, guard her! Lance thought as he steered Infinity in front of his sister.

"Why does that dragon smell like a human?" growled the horned dragon. "It is unnatural."

"Because I am a human!" said Zoe triumphantly. "Or sort of. I was a human. But now I am a dragon!"

"She is an abomination," sneered the small whiskered dragon. "She represents everything wrong with humans and dragons coexisting. There has not been a shape-shifter like this ever! It cannot be!"

"And yet here she is. A human girl in dragon form," said Violet. "Turned by golden elixir. And if you think she is an abomination, you must have no idea what is coming."

This got the three dragons' attention. "What do you speak of?"

"We speak of the Devourer," said Neon. "He is coming. And he does not care if you are dragon or human, only that you can be drained of your power, of your life, of your essence. He will devour us all."

"The Devourer is not real," said the horned dragon, but Lance saw how its eyes darted nervously.

"He is as real as you and me. We have seen what he has sent ahead. We have seen the Petrifiers." Jaws relayed to these three dragons everything that had happened, and slowly they began to look more intrigued, and then alarmed as they realized what was to come.

"What is it you want from us, then? We will not side with humans. Even against a shared enemy," said the whiskered dragon.

"You do not need to help us. But do not stop us from our quest," said Infinity. It was the first time she had spoken aloud to the three green dragons, and she spoke with a quiet authority that Lance had never heard. "We seek the blood-berry tree."

"It is protected," said the horned dragon.

"We must reach it," said Infinity. "All of the New World, including Dracordia and its dragons who hate humans, depends on it."

The three dragons exchanged a sly look. "Then seek it. You know the legends. It lies somewhere on the Lake of Life."

"You know where the blood-berry tree is, don't you?" said Lance. "But you won't help us."

"Do not speak to us unless you are invited to speak," snapped the whiskered dragon. "We have no interest in what humans have to say."

"You have to help us!" said Lance, feeling suddenly on the verge of tears. They had come so far and battled so much. "Please!"

Try your erhu, urged Infinity. *Even these grumpy dragons will hear the truth in your music.*

Lance quickly unstrung his erhu from his back and started to play. He poured himself into the song, trying to make their plight clear to these dragons.

When he was finished, the dragons stared at him.

"Your power is in your music," said the whiskered one.

"And now we know you do not only ride with dragons, but with the Infinite Dragon," added the diamond-spiked dragon, assessing Infinity.

"We will not fight the Infinite Dragon, for we know the prophecy," said the horned dragon, who exchanged a look with the others before turning back to Lance and Infinity. "We will guide you. If you do reach the blood-berry tree, know that it will not give up its berries freely. We have been trying for longer than you humans have been alive."

The whiskered dragon blew a great plume of smoke that arced across the lake.

"Follow that," it said. "The smoke will lead you."

"Thank you," said Lance.

"Do not forget that we have helped you," said the

whiskered dragon. "And if you do manage to take the blood berries, keep one for us."

Lance nodded solemnly.

"Then I hope we meet again," said the horned dragon, and as one, the three green dragons dived down into the water, leaving behind nothing but the smoke trail that would supposedly take them to the blood-berry tree.

"Do we trust them?" said Lance.

"Or is it a trap?" said Arthur warily.

"I trust them," said Infinity. "I could read their hearts, and while they truly dislike humans, Lance convinced them with his music that the New World is worth saving and that I am the key to saving it."

"Then follow that smoke trail," said Lance, and he and Infinity led the way.

Buried Alive

The Lake of Life was so vast that it felt almost endless. Lance lost track of time as they flew across it, following the smoke trail until finally he spotted a small, circular island. As they drew closer, he noted how the edge was dense with vegetation but the center was a tangled dome of bare branches and spiky thorns that was as large as a circus tent. Lance didn't see a single berry.

The others, who were hovering next to Lance and Infinity, all stared at the thorny mass in front of them. "Is this it?" said Lance, trying not to sound disappointed. "This doesn't even look like a tree! It looks like a thorny thicket! And where are the berries?"

Arthur furrowed his brow in concentration. "The blood-berry tree is in there," said Arthur. "I think these branches may even be part of the tree itself. Like the outer shell. But I can see the berries in my mind, and they are somewhere inside that tangle of branches."

"Neon, I want to take a closer look," said Bea, and they flew down to the center of the island. Bea inspected one of the branches, her fingers outstretched and shooting small sparks of green lightning. Bea frowned. "That is strange." She leaned in closer to the branch she'd zapped and raised a finger, firing one more spark of lightning at it. The lightning struck the branch, and the branch seemed to absorb the energy. Bea's frown deepened. "My molecule magic doesn't work on these branches. I sense that they are indestructible. I think the only way we're going to get in is by squeezing our way between the branches."

"Nonsense," rumbled Jaws. "No branch can withstand my strength." He unhinged his jaws, revealing rows of jagged teeth as sharp as knives, and bit down on a large section of the thicket.

Jaws's eyes were wide with surprise when the branches didn't snap like twigs. In fact, the branches didn't move at all. They stayed perfectly tangled as if they were made from stone. Jaws growled, his mouth quivering as he bit down harder on the branches.

"You can do it, Jaws," said Arthur, and Lance knew his friend was sending his dragon strength through their heart-bond.

Jaws grunted, and his whole body strained with effort, but the branches did not break.

"It is no use, Jaws," Neon said, as he watched with interest. "We should save our strength."

Jaws released his bite on the branches, which remained perfectly in place, and roared, shooting a fireball at the thicket. But once again, the flames passed right through the thorny branches with little effect.

"Is your mouth okay?" Lance asked. "Those thorns look sharp."

"My mouth is fine," grumbled Jaws. "It is only my pride that is wounded."

"The all-powerful Jaws," Violet mocked, her lips curled up in a half smile. "Stronger than everything in all of the worlds, except some branches."

"Now that Jaws has proven my point," said Bea,

"we need to figure out how we are going to get through these thorns."

"The dragons are way too big," Arthur pointed out.

"But we aren't," said Lance slowly as the idea crystalized in his mind. "And our new super-suits will protect us from the thorns, right, Bea?"

Bea nodded.

"What about me?" said Zoe, slipping off Violet's back and hovering in the air, her small wings beating rapidly. "I'm small enough to fit through! And I have dragon scales now!"

"But we do not know what is in there," said Neon. "And we know we are strongest together."

"It is the only way," Lance argued. "We have to get those berries." He looked at each of the dragons in turn. "You have to trust us."

"You are all very brave," said Infinity, and Lance felt her pride through their bond.

"I don't feel very brave," Arthur admitted. "But I agree with Lance—this is the only way. And at least the four of us will be together."

"And we'll still all be connected through our heart-bonds," added Bea.

Jaws let out a huff. "Fine. But be careful!"

"Arthur," said Lance. "Can you see a way in?"

Arthur put his finger to his temple as he focused. "If we go to the base of the thicket, there is a small crawl space. I see a path to the center from there."

"Be careful," rumbled Neon, "and remember this is Dracordia—danger is everywhere. If you get in trouble, get out as fast as possible."

Lance, Bea, and Arthur leaped off their dragons' backs and floated to the ground at the base of the dome thicket. Zoe flew down next to them, and again Lance was struck by how strange it was to see his sister as a dragon. She caught him staring and stuck out her tongue.

"Before we go in," said Lance, "let me try one thing." He pulled out his erhu and struck a branch with it like a hammer. The erhu recoiled back, nearly flying out of his hand, the branch remaining as still as a statue.

Lance shrugged at his friends. "Just checking."

Bea rolled her eyes. "Of course you had to try whacking it."

"Come on, you guys, follow me!" said Arthur. "And, Zoe, watch out for your tail!"

The group crawled through the thicket like it was a jungle gym, dipping and twisting, their supersuits or scales protecting them from the thorns. As they made their way deeper into the thicket, Lance thought of the times when he and Zoe had taken shortcuts on the way home from school through the thickest, untracked parts of the woods. It had always been Zoe's idea, of course, and Lance would agree, even though he knew the "shortcut" would end up taking them longer. Lance watched as Zoe easily moved through the thorny thicket with short, quick movements. He drew comfort from the fact that Zoe still moved like Zoe, even if she was a dragon now. She had always loved the woods, and exploring. Lance wondered if that was why Violet had sought them out that day in the woods, if through her bond with Zoe she had sensed Zoe's joy and sense of adventure. It seemed so long ago now, but Lance still remembered his feeling of awe when Violet had appeared to them, and when he had seen the gold charge run between Violet's and Zoe's hearts—the proof of their heart-bond. So much had happened since then. Lance knew that if they ever did make it back home to New London, both he and his sister would be different from before.

He just hoped Zoe would be back in her human form by then.

The thicket grew darker as they made their way deeper into its core. "Torches on," said Bea, and their suits lit up the path in front of them. Progress was difficult at first, and Zoe needed Lance to push her through a particularly tight opening, but to Lance's relief, the branches of the thicket thinned as they went deeper.

They kept going until they emerged in a small clearing that was shaped like the inside of a dome. The first thing Lance noticed were dozens of vines dangling from overhead, so low that they almost touched the ground. The vines were as thick as pythons, and they swung gently from side to side despite the still air.

At the center of the clearing was a large tree trunk that went from the ground all the way up to the branches overhead. Thick, exposed roots twisted out of the ground, connecting to the base of the tree. Lance was shocked when a burst of fluorescent green light pulsed from the roots and into the base of the tree, lighting it up from the inside. The burst of light flowed up the tree's trunk, like blood through veins, before flowing back down the vines and the branches along the inner wall of the dome. Everything in the clearing swayed gently back and forth to the rhythm of the pulsing tree.

"The thicket *is* the tree," said Lance in awe. "Its branches grow out around it like a protective shell."

"So, what we were crawling through were its outer branches?" asked Zoe.

"I think so," said Lance. And then he saw it. "Look!" He pointed to the top of a hanging vine, which was dotted with small red fruit. They were plump with strands of thread hanging from their skin, and each time the tree pulsed with green light, the threads floated up and down like the tentacles of a jellyfish. Lance looked at the other vines and saw that all of them bore the plump red berries. "The berries are at the top of the vines!"

"Woo-hoo!" cried Zoe. "Let's grab some and get out of here," she said as she zipped toward one of the vines.

"Wait!" cried Lance. He could sense with his enhanced awareness from the super-suit that they weren't alone. He looked up and saw two shapes swooping down at Zoe. "Watch out, Zoe!" Lance leaped into the air at one of the creatures, crashing into it and tackling it to the ground. Now that he was right on top of it, he realized it was like a giant bat.

"Oh no, you don't!" cried Bea, raising a hand to her helmet and shooting a beam from her visor that struck the other creature square in the chest, knocking it to the ground as well.

Lance wrestled with the bat-like creature as it frantically flapped its wings. He maneuvered himself onto its back and wrapped his arm around its neck, putting it in a headlock.

"Let go of my love!" cried the other creature, who had gotten to its feet. But as it leaped in the air, Bea shot it with another beam, holding it in place. Lance could see Bea straining with effort as she held it back.

The bat-like creatures were about the same size as Lance. Each of their foreheads bulged with three small red eyes. At the center of each face was a large snout that came to a point at the top. They had gaping mouths packed with sharp teeth. The two creatures looked nearly identical except that the one Bea held in place had one ear that flopped over one of its eyes.

The creature Lance was holding squirmed, and Lance tightened his grip around its neck. As he squeezed, a long tongue rolled out of its mouth. "Let me go," the bat-creature squawked.

"Only if you leave us alone," said Lance.

The creature continued to squirm in his arms, and then it flung its long tongue upward, the tip of it flipping open Lance's visor and licking his eyeball.

"Argh!" cried Lance, releasing the bat-creature.

The creature scurried away, flying back up to the top of the clearing.

"Let me go!" cried the other bat-creature, who was still caught in Bea's beam. It shrieked, letting out an ear-splitting screech that made Lance flinch. It shook free and joined the other bat-creature at the top of the clearing.

"Leave us and we won't hurt you," said Arthur.

"Very well," replied the one with the floppy ear.

It turned to the other bat-creature. "Let them find out for themselves. We can snack on what's left of them later."

The other bat-creature flicked its tongue into its nose and licked its lips in one fluid motion. "Yum. What a delightful idea. Enjoy you later, humans. And strange dragon-human." The two creatures flew up and out of the clearing.

Zoe fluttered over to Lance. "Thanks for looking out for me."

Lance gave her a smile.

"Now can we pick the blood berries?" Zoe asked.

"That was a bit of an ominous warning from those bat-creatures," said Bea. "Is there something we're missing?"

"There's only one way to find out," said Arthur, leaping to the top of the clearing. He grabbed on to a hanging vine and pointed at one of its berries. "Shall I do the honors?"

"Wait!" cried Lance. "Let's not rush into this."

"I can't explain it, but I can sense that the tree wants to share its berries with me." And Arthur plucked a fruit from its stem.

The group held their breath.

The tree continued to pulse. Once. Twice. Three times.

"Seems okay to me," Arthur said, as he plucked two more berries from the vine.

"Good job listening to the tree and trusting your instincts," said Bea.

"Catch," Arthur called down as he tossed three berries—one to each of his friends.

Lance, Zoe, and Bea caught the berries and inspected them.

"This is the coolest berry I've ever seen," said Zoe, holding it up to her face and smelling it.

Lance brought his berry close to his face. "I wonder what—?"

Before Lance could finish his thought, the ground started to rumble. The pulses of green light from the roots quickened, faster and faster and faster, until the tree and all its roots and branches were a solid fluorescent green. And then the roots unshackled themselves from the ground and reached out at them like arms.

Lance dashed toward Zoe and pushed her away,

just as a root was about to close itself around her. The root took Lance in her place, wrapping itself around him like an anaconda.

"Lance!" yelled Zoe, flying toward him, but another root snatched her out of the air.

"Bea! Watch out!" cried Arthur, who leaped down from above and began tugging at another root that had captured Bea. "Let her go!"

The branch around Lance tightened its grip, squeezing the air out of him. He tried his hardest to break free, but the roots only gripped harder the more he fought. If these roots were as strong as the branches in the thicket, he couldn't see how he would find a way to break free. Lance heard Bea let out a yell as the root around her tightened its grip as well.

And then the roots started to lower themselves back into the soil, with Lance, Zoe, and Bea still trapped in their coils.

"We're going to be buried alive!" choked Zoe, who was struggling for air and already halfway into the earth.

Lance tried to yell, but the root had squeezed all

the air out of him. Lower and lower it went, plunging him into the earth.

"Let go of my friends!" Arthur cried again.

Lance looked to Arthur and was surprised to see that he was still trying to pull Bea back out of the ground. The roots seemed unbothered by his presence and were completely ignoring him, even as they tried to strangle Lance, Bea, and Zoe.

Arthur ran over to Lance and wrapped his arms around the root holding him. He pulled up with all of his might. "LET! HIM! GO!" he yelled between tugs. But it was no use. The root yanked Lance deeper into the soil. He was almost up to his neck now. This was it. This was how it was going to end.

"Help!" Zoe screamed, straining her neck to keep it above ground.

Her cries pierced Lance's heart like a skewer. He couldn't let his sister down. He had to figure a way out. Why weren't the roots going for Arthur? *There must be something he's done differently*, Lance thought frantically. Was it his power? Did his pathfinding ability make him immune to the blood-berry tree in some way?

And then Lance got an idea. Blood. Arthur was

the only one who had given his blood to the tree.

"Take ... my ... blood," he huffed, barely louder than a whisper.

The root holding Lance instantly loosened its grip and pushed him back out of the ground.

It worked!

"Tell the tree that you'll give it your blood!"

Lance saw Zoe and Bea mouth the words, and to his relief the tree lifted them back into the air and placed them on either side of Lance.

A thorny branch slunk down from the dome above and hovered in front of the group expectantly.

Lance peeled his glove back and pressed an exposed finger to one of its thorns. A drop of blood fell to the ground. Bea and Zoe did the same. As their drops of blood sank into the soil, the fluorescent green light started to pulse again. Fast at first, before settling into the same slow, calming rhythm that they had first seen when they'd entered the clearing.

"You saved us," said Bea, running over to Lance and throwing her arms around him.

"You're the best," said Zoe, wrapping them both in her dragon arms.

"That was amazing," said Arthur. "How did you figure that out?"

Lance shrugged. "The roots weren't going for you, and I knew it must have been something you'd done that we hadn't. And they only started to attack when *we* touched the berries, not you. When I thought about your pathfinding power to find the tree, I thought about how you gave it a drop of your blood."

"Brilliant," said Bea. "The tree must only let you take its berries if you've offered it your blood in return."

"What a weird tree," said Arthur.

"Let's get these berries and get out of here," said Zoe.

20

The Maze in the Sky

Bea revealed a backpack she had tucked away in her suit, and they stuffed it with as many berries as they could manage before heading back through the thicket to their dragons.

"You have proven yourselves more than worthy to be a part of the Dragon Force," said Neon after Zoe recounted what had happened.

Jaws nodded. "I can sense the four of you getting stronger and more confident. Your powers are growing with every challenge that we face. As are your bonds with one another."

"You have made us very proud," said Neon. "But now is not the time for celebration. Now is the time that we will be truly tested."

"The greatest test the Dragon Force has ever had," Jaws added.

"Time to save the world," said Bea, grinning. "No big deal."

"Are we ready?" Lance asked.

"Ready as we'll ever be," said Zoe.

Bea took a single blood berry from her backpack and tossed it to the ground. "Ready," she said.

Lance gave her a confused look.

"For those grumpy green dragons," Bea replied. "We said we'd leave them a berry if we succeeded, and I don't like breaking promises."

"Plus those looked like the type of dragons that would hold a grudge," Arthur added. "And we've got enough enemies as it is."

"Good thinking," said Lance as he pulled out his erhu. "Anything else before we fly to the Devourer's Den?"

"We are as prepared as we will ever be. It is time," said Infinity with a flap of her wings. "Lance, call to the stars to show us the way."

Lance nodded at his dragon as he took out his erhu. Playing string instruments had always come naturally to Lance. He loved to play the classics, but he also loved to make his own versions of songs he heard on the radio. But what he loved most of all was playing melodies that simply came to him. He would start with a familiar refrain that he knew and then build on it, moving notes around, stacking them together, to make the music that spoke to his heart. He supposed what he did with music was similar to what Bea did with molecules. And with his power, he found he could play any tune he wanted on his erhu as if he were singing it with his own voice. Now he sang to the stars through his erhu. He asked them to guide their way to the Devourer's Den.

As he played, Lance felt the scar in his left hand throb. A gentle prickle at first, and then it began to glow. Lance could feel a power growing in his palm. As he played his erhu, his palm grew brighter until there was so much energy that Lance had to squeeze his hand into a fist to contain it. His hand shook with effort. And then he pointed his palm away from him and opened his hand. A burst of stardust shot out from the scar, illuminating a path up into the sky.

Lance smiled. "Follow me." He leaped up on Infinity's back, and the others did the same with their dragons.

Lance led the group into the sky, following the trail of stardust. As they went higher, Lance realized that the trail didn't go in a straight line, but in an intricate pattern. It looped round and round, sometimes back on itself. It was as if they were doing a dance through the sky. Rolling, spinning, and doing figure eights and half-loops. Every now and again they would fly through what looked to Lance like a wrinkle in the air. A wrinkle that, if you weren't paying close attention, would have been indistinguishable from the sky around it. The light hit it differently, and it was a strange shade of blue. When they flew through it, the landscape down below would change, as if they'd found a secret passage. Snowy mountains, barren desert, impossibly tall forests. The group zoomed on and on. They had just flown through a wrinkle in the sky when a choppy sea appeared beneath them. The stardust trail bent downward into the sea, and so Lance dived, straight down, following its path.

They flew through the surface of the sea but

instead of being submerged in water, Lance found they were back in the blue sky, soaring higher and higher. Then a swirling white portal formed above them, the trail of stardust piercing its center. Lance led them into the portal, and they found themselves in a dark night sky. The stardust had vanished. In front of them was a giant circular cloud, so large and perfectly round that it looked like a moon.

"Well done, Lance," said Neon. "It appears you have succeeded in leading us to the Devourer's Den."

"That was amazing," said Arthur. "I could barely keep up with my pathfinding power. The path we were making in the sky was like a key opening a lock."

"I did not know that portals could be opened in that way," said Jaws.

"The stars know much more than even us," said Violet.

"I can't believe we made it. That this really is the Devourer's Den," said Arthur.

"It kind of looks like a giant cotton ball in space," said Zoe, peering up at the cloud.

"The star said it would look like a normal cloud,

but it is poisonous mist," Infinity warned.

"I think that our suits might protect us from the mist," said Bea as she flew with Neon to inspect the mist closer. She frowned. "But that doesn't help our dragons."

Violet flew next to Bea and inspected the cloud. "Mist is my speciality." She flicked her tongue out and dipped the tip of it into the cloud as if tasting it. "Ugh," she snorted. "Nasty stuff." She shook her head as if shaking the taste from her mouth. "But nothing I can't handle." She closed her eyes and twisted her long, slender body from side to side, her scales flapping up and down on her body like swinging doors. As the scales moved, they released a translucent mist, almost like steam, that formed a sphere around the group like a protective bubble. Violet opened her eyes and flew closer to the cloud, and the protective bubble floated forward with her. As the surface of the bubble pressed into the cloud, the fog from the cloud dispersed, revealing a wall of bones held together by ice. "The poisonous cloud can't get in this bubble, so we will be safe as long as we are inside it."

"I knew you could do it!" said Zoe, her butterfly

wings flapping in the air. "Now all we have to do is figure out how to get in."

"Let me see what I can do," said Arthur, bringing his hands to his temples in his signature pose. A few moments passed before Arthur looked back up at the group. "It's a complicated maze to get in, but I think I can do it."

"Show us the way," said Lance.

Arthur nodded and flew with Jaws to the bottom of the protective bubble. "Violet, follow me."

Arthur led the group to the very bottom of the cloud. The edge of the protective bubble overlapped with the cloud as they flew, revealing the bones and ice behind its fog. When they stopped, Arthur flew up to the wall of bones and ice and ran his hand along its surface before gripping the pointed end of a large claw. With a tug, Arthur pulled it out of the ice. He turned the claw around, so that the sharp point faced the wall, and pushed it back into the same hole. The wall began to shake, and after a moment, the ice around the claw melted and the bones fell out of the sky into the nothingness below them, revealing a large tunnel.

"This is the way in," said Arthur.

"Everyone, be on guard," said Neon.

The group followed Arthur and Jaws through the entrance.

"This is creepy," said Zoe, looking at the walls around her, all made of bones and ice.

"Stay alert!" said Lance.

"I'm always alert," said Zoe, whacking Lance with her tail.

"Hey!" said Arthur. "Keep up!"

They flew deeper into the Devourer's Den, the air getting colder and colder. Flecks of frost were appearing as if the air itself was starting to freeze.

After a few minutes, the group came to a fork in the tunnel. "This way," said Arthur, leading them to the right. It was the first of many turns through which Arthur navigated them—so many that Lance lost track.

"You'd better not get petrified, or there's no way we're getting back out of here," Lance joked.

"We really would be lost without you," Bea added.

Arthur grinned. "We're almost there."

After a few more bends, the group came to a dead

end. The wall was not notably different from the other walls they had seen except that a giant skull of a dragon jutted out from its center, the dragon's hollow eyes gazing blankly at them.

Arthur floated off Jaws's back and reached both his hands out, putting one fist into each of the skull's nostrils. With a quick tug, he pulled the dragon skull out of the wall. The ice in the wall melted away and the bones fell to the floor, revealing a wall of black smoke.

"The Devourer's Den is on the other side of this smoke," said Arthur. "Are we sure we're ready for this?"

"Ready as I'll ever be," said Zoe.

"Remember," said Lance, "keep the fear out. Be brave."

"If we don't speak again," said Neon, "know that I am proud of all of you and grateful to have had you in my life."

"Don't be so dramatic," said Bea affectionately. "We'll be fine!"

Jaws ran his large tongue over Arthur's face, leaving a trail of drool. "You are a good human, Arthur."

Arthur wiped the spit from his face as he returned to Jaws's back, and Lance could see that he was smiling.

Lance felt a warmth from Infinity that surrounded him like a hug. *You have given me purpose beyond the prophecy*, she said to him down their bond. *And that is the greatest gift I could have received. My whole life I have felt the weight of the prophecy, of being the one who will save the realms. It was my sole purpose. But you have opened my heart. Whatever happens on the other side of this wall, know that I am always your dragon. I will always be in your heart, just as you will always be in mine. You are my infinity.*

Lance placed a hand behind his dragon's ear.

Always, he replied, his heart full.

Lance turned to the rest of the group. "Infinity and I will lead the way." And then they flew through the fog and into the Devourer's Den.

The Heart of the Dragon Force

They burst into the center of the Devourer's Den, and Lance gasped.

All around them were hundreds of humans and dragons, all floating among the bones and ice. And they were petrified, their eyes glazed over, their bodies as stiff as stone. Lance's own blood ran cold. He knew what petrified creatures looked like—he'd seen Kronos—but to see all these dragons and humans frozen in such a vulnerable state chilled him to the bone. At least they had found the den, he reasoned. Now they could fix it—now they could save the others.

Lance saw Spark, the magnificent blue dragon who was heart-bonded with Billy Chan, leader of the Dragon Force, and everything about seeing her petrified felt wrong. Her neck was bent strangely, as if she had been struggling in the moment she had been petrified. And still astride her back was a petrified Billy Chan. He was holding on with just his legs, tilted to the side, and one of his hands was outstretched, as if he had been trying to stop an oncoming attacker. Lance wanted to fly right up to him and unpetrify him, but he knew he had to stay focused. There were certainly Petrifiers hiding here in the den, and they had to deal with them first.

"Where are the Petrifiers?" whispered Arthur, clearly thinking the same thing as Lance.

"They must be here somewhere," said Lance. "Be on your guard."

Suddenly, a dozen Petrifiers, all in different forms, swooped in from the edges of the den. They howled and whooped—bats, bears, wolves—all striking fear in Lance's heart.

"Remember!" cried Lance. "We can master our own fears! Do not let them in! Shine the fear back on them! They cannot face fear themselves!" Lance desperately hoped this was true. It was what the Swarm had said, what the Mirage had promised. And they each now had some of the Mirage's shimmery essence with them. This was what they could use to reflect back the fear—this was how they could petrify the Petrifiers.

Lance braced himself as he prepared to face his fears in the best way he knew how: through his music.

He began to play his erhu as one Petrifier, in the form of a snarling two-headed wolf made of smoke and shadow and with glowing red eyes, tried to latch onto his arm. Lance's song came out in spurts as he could not focus on what he wanted to play, his fear pulling him out of his rhythm.

Lance felt the fear begin to spread inside him and he pushed it back. He was stronger than his fears, and he had not come this far only to fall now. He had survived so much; he had battled the Swarm and won; he had been swallowed by a shark-dragon, taken down the flying krakens. And he had faced the worst of his fears in the Mirage and proven that he would do anything to protect those he cared about.

And right now, he needed to summon that courage, because everything depended on it. He was not afraid.

"See yourself and feel your own fear!" he shouted at the Petrifier. Lance felt the Mirage magic begin to shimmer to life in his suit, in his song, and reflect the Petrifier back at itself.

The two-headed shadow wolf gave a yelp as it stared at Lance's shimmering suit and at the reflective magic of the Mirage bouncing back at it. Suddenly the shadows and smoke that it was made of hardened, like water turning into ice, and the light went out of its eyes.

Lance looked at it and felt no fear.

You did it! Infinity's pride washed over him. *You mastered your fear and turned it back on the Petrifier!*

The newly petrified Petrifier floated up and bumped into another member of the Dragon Force who had been petrified.

"Lance! That was awesome!" called Arthur from across the den. "Now I know how to do it too!" He turned directly toward an oncoming Petrifier and howled at it, not in fear but in triumph. Lance watched as Arthur's super-suit shimmered in Mirage magic, and the Petrifier that had been attacking him froze in midair. Lance realized they were all summoning the Mirage-reflecting magic in different ways. Lance channeled his courage in his music, and Arthur howled his rage and fear—letting it pour out of him and onto the attacking Petrifier.

"Whoop! We've got this!" yelled Bea, thrusting her hands out at another Petrifier swooping toward her, this one in the shape of a bat. "SEE YOURSELF AND FEEL THE FEAR YOU CAUSE!" The Petrifier bat blinked and then immediately hardened into stone.

"Let me try!" cried Zoe. Lance and Infinity flew to her side. Lance was nervous because while Zoe still had some semblance of her super-suit on over her dragon scales, what if the reflecting magic didn't work the same way it had for him and Bea and Arthur? Then, as a rampaging Petrifier in the shape of an angry bull charged at Zoe, all of her scales shimmered like a liquid mirror, and the Petrifier stopped, stunned. "Nothing scares me anymore!" Zoe screamed, and Lance heard how she had conquered her fear in that cry. "Now *you* feel the fear I felt when I turned into a dragon, feel the fear when I thought I would be separated from my family forever, feel every drop of fear that has ever coursed through me!" Her cry echoed all around them, and the Petrifier hardened to stone, floating away to a distant part of the den.

The Petrifiers were in chaos, unable to process what was happening to them. They kept coming, seeping out of the walls of the den, through the bones and ice, but now Lance, Bea, Arthur, and Zoe knew how to fight back.

So did their dragons.

Violet was zooming around the den, her scales shimmering with Mirage-reflecting magic at every Petrifier she passed. She was so fast, and so fearless, that all she had to do was fly past them for them to be petrified.

Neon was crackling with his own electric energy, and bursts of the reflective Mirage magic shone out from his horns, creating mystic mirrors in the air that blocked the Petrifiers inside them.

Jaws roared, his fearlessness echoing all around

them, and the sound waves transformed into reflective magic, crashing over the Petrifiers as they continued their onslaught.

But they had met their match.

"Yes!" yelled Lance with a fist pump.

"Lance," said Infinity quickly, and sounding frantic. "Do not get overconfident. We still must unpetrify the others before the Devourer arrives. And he will be here soon. I can feel it."

"We can use the same magic against the Devourer!" said Lance. He felt invincible. "We know how to beat him now! Isn't he just like a giant Petrifier?"

But Infinity's fear rolled off her, so much so that Lance was worried it would attract a Petrifier. "The Petrifiers are mere particles of him," said the dragon. "His power is far greater than that. I do not know if the Mirage magic will work on a creature of such magnitude and vastness. We will need every last member of the Dragon Force." She was beginning to tremble. "The Devourer can sense what is happening to his Petrifiers, and it is making him angry. I can feel it. And he is close. We must stay focused, and we must unpetrify the rest of the Dragon Force before he arrives!"

"Dragons!" shouted Lance. "You keep petrifying the Petrifiers!" He leaped off Infinity and found he was able to glide and float through the air. He knew part of that was because of the enhanced super-suit, thanks to Bea, and part of it was because there was less gravity here in the Devourer's Den. "We'll start using the blood berries to unpetrify the Dragon Force!"

Lance swam through the air toward Spark and Billy Chan.

He took one of the blood berries and cracked it open. There were dozens of blood-red seeds inside it. Lance carefully extracted one of the seeds and pressed it into Billy's petrified palm.

The blood-berry seed lit up for a moment and then sank into Billy's palm.

A moment later, Billy's hand twitched. And then he blinked.

"Lance Lo?" he said, his voice coming out a croak. "Have you come to save the Dragon Force?"

"Not just me," said Lance, beaming at his hero. He gestured back to where his friends were unpetrifying the rest of the Dragon Force.

Billy stretched his arms over his head. "Lance, this is amazing. *You* are amazing." Lance's smile grew even wider. "All right," Billy went on, still stretching. "Now tell me how to unpetrify my dragon!"

Lance handed Billy one of the blood berries. "Use the seed!" he said. "When it touches the skin, it will sink in and do its magic."

"Incredible," said Billy. He pressed one of the seeds on Spark's back, between her wings, and a moment later her eyes shone and her wings flapped to life.

"It feels nice to move again," she said, and Billy let out a joyful laugh. Then Spark looked at Lance. "I assume I have you to thank for this, young Lance Lo."

Lance felt as if Spark was seeing into his very soul. "I just did what any Dragon Force member would do," he said.

"Few could have achieved what you and your friends have," said Spark. Then her eyes glowed bright, and electricity began to spark all over her. "Billy, I have had a vision of the Devourer. He is close. And he is ravenous. The vision is hazy, but I can sense his nearness."

Spark turned to Lance, her voice softening. "And I have seen just how brave Lance and the other young recruits have been. We are very lucky they arrived when they did."

Lance gaped at Spark. "How do you know all that?"

"Spark is a seer dragon," Billy explained. "Sometimes her power means she has visions of the future, but she can also see into the past. And because we're linked through our heart-bond, she's sent me the visions, so I'm all caught up. And she's right—you have been incredibly brave." He tilted his head. "What I didn't see is how you and your friends learned how to float in midair."

Lance grinned again. "The gravity is different here in the den. It's why everyone petrified was floating too."

Billy took a tentative step off Spark and grinned as he hovered in the air, but not quite as effortlessly as Lance. He flapped his arms, and Spark ducked under him, reseating Billy on her back. "How come it is so easy for you?" he said.

Lance cleared his throat. "Oh and . . . Bea upgraded the super-suits. I hope that is okay!"

Billy laughed again. "Upgraded super-suits? You four are the most impressive bunch of recruits we've ever had!"

"They remind me of you and your friends, Billy," said Spark, and Lance glowed with pride at the comparison.

"The heart of the Dragon Force has always been the bond between the members and their dragons and the bravery they show together," said Billy. "Lance Lo, you have proven that you were meant to be in the Dragon Force. Thanks to you and your friends, we'll be able to win this."

Lance was so overwhelmed by Billy's words, all he could do was nod.

Billy grinned at Lance. "Now. How about we unpetrify everyone else? I have a few friends who might be able to speed up the process a bit."

He leaped over to where Lola Lam, one of the elite members of the Dragon Force, was petrified next to her dragon, Neptune. A moment later, Lola was unpetrified. Lance wondered why Billy had chosen to unpetrify Lola first, but then he remembered Lola's power.

Lola had the ability to stop time itself and move around while others were frozen in a moment. She would be the perfect person to unpetrify everyone. "Lola, I'll explain everything in a minute, but right now I need a time-stop," said Billy. "Keep me in the time-stop with you, and we are going to use these blood berries to unpetrify everyone."

Lola frowned in confusion. "Blood berries?"

"I'll explain later," said Billy. "We are running out of time."

Lola smirked. "I'm never running out of time. You can tell me in the time-stop." She grabbed Billy's hand and began to crackle with power.

Lance felt a blast of power wash over him, which he assumed was from Lola, and a moment later he saw the rest of the Dragon Force members and their dragons shudder back to life.

They had done it. They had saved the Dragon Force.

There were still Petrifiers coming through the bone walls of the den, but Lance and the others knew now how to stop them. Neon made reflective cages in increasing sizes that caught the Petrifiers in droves.

"All right, everyone," Billy shouted, his voice

echoing off the walls of the den. "Glad to see you all moving again. I'm sure you have questions, but right now we do what we do best—work together as a team! We won't let these Petrifiers get the best of us again! Remember, they can't petrify you if you master your fear! The Devourer will be here soon, so be ready to fight! This will be unlike anything we've faced before, so we must be prepared for anything. We can do it!"

The Dragon Force let out a cheer, which was so full of courage that an oncoming Petrifier froze simply from hearing it.

Knowing that Billy believed in them made Lance feel as if he could do anything. As if he could single-handedly defeat the Devourer.

But as the Dragon Force now easily stopped the Petrifiers, Lance kept feeling Infinity's fear. It was so strong, he was worried that she would attract a Petrifier.

Lance floated over to her. "Infinity? What is it?"

Infinity began to glow gold, and Lance knew she was trying to level up for something. The gold flashed and flickered, like a lightbulb trying to turn on. Whatever she was attempting to do, she wasn't managing. Then there was a burst of gold light so bright that Lance had to close his eyes. When he opened them, the entire den was washed in golden light, and he saw that it was pouring out of the cracks and into the sky beyond. He knew Infinity was using it to seek out the Devourer, maybe even trying to hold him back. Then Infinity shuddered and locked eyes with Lance. He knew with a sudden, sickening certainty what she was going to say. And even though this moment had been inevitable, he still didn't feel ready.

"The Devourer has arrived."

The Devourer

A deep growl shook the entire den.

Lance realized that the Devourer's Den was not a place for the Devourer to take refuge in, like a fox or a wolf.

As the top of the den was ripped off, like someone taking the lid from a jar of honey, two enormous glowing white eyes gazed in at them, and the truth hit Lance.

The stars may have called this a den, but it was a den for the Petrifiers and for the petrified.

To the Devourer, the den was a jar. A bowl.

His Petrifiers had prepared him a feast, and even put them on a plate. And while the Dragon Force might not be petrified any longer, they were still trapped here inside the den.

They should not have stayed here in the den—they should have left while they'd had the chance, Lance thought to himself. They had been celebrating their win over the Petrifiers, but that clearly meant nothing in the grand scheme of things.

"You all smell delicious." The Devourer's voice bored into Lance's skull, into his bones. "What a merry chase this has been. I cannot recall the last time I had this much fun on a hunt."

Lance began to quake with fear. *Master your fear*, he told himself, *do not give in*. It was hard to feel brave, though, when even the dragons looked small next to the Devourer.

Lance himself was no bigger than the tip of one of his claws. The Devourer could reach in and scoop up all of the humans like grabbing a handful of chips. Lance could only see the Devourer's eyes peering in at them, the tips of two of his claws hanging on the edges of the den, ready to rip it open even farther. The Devourer was made of smoke and shadow somehow made solid. He had long fur, like a wolf, and wolf-like ears, too. Lance suspected if he could see his snout, it would also resemble a wolf's. But the scale of the Devourer was enormous, and there was something strangely ... manlike about him too. Especially his claws, which did not seem like the claws of a wolf or a beast, but like human hands with monstrously long nails.

The Devourer inhaled again. "Truly delicious. I will start by drinking all of the magic here, and then I will finish by crunching on your very bones, and then of course when I have grown even stronger, I will devour your entire world."

"You'll have to get past us first!" yelled Billy Chan, and he and Spark zoomed up toward the Devourer's face with a burst of light and power.

The Devourer began to laugh, and as Billy and Spark drew closer, he snarled at them and then moved so his giant snout was practically in the den, blowing them away with an effortless puff.

Spark pinwheeled back into the den with a *thump*.

Lola Lam and her dragon, the giant Neptune, sprang into action. But even Neptune, the biggest dragon Lance had ever seen, looked small next to the Devourer. Lance hoped that Lola's time-stopping power would be enough to defeat the Devourer.

As Lola began to glow, Lance wondered if she had done it—if she had frozen time and figured out how to stop the Devourer—but nothing had happened.

Panic flashed across Lola's face, and Lance's heart sank.

"A valiant effort indeed, but I am from another universe," said the Devourer. "Time has no bearing on me. Your so-called power to slow time will not work."

With a mighty roar, Neptune sent out one of her famous sound blasts straight at the Devourer. The creature opened his colossal mouth—a mouth big enough to swallow the entire den and everyone in it in one gulp if he wanted. The Devourer drank up the power blast and licked his lips. "Delicious, as I thought." Then he howled again, shaking the entire den.

The rest of the Dragon Force all tried their various attacks, but nothing worked. If anything, it all seemed to be making the Devourer stronger. The legendary Dragon Force member Charlotte Bell, riding her colossal red dragon, Tank, charged at the Devourer as Tank breathed out streams of blazing hot fire.

The Devourer simply drank it up. The fire had no effect on him.

"MORE!" the Devourer roared at them, so loudly that the den shook again. "I WANT IT ALL!"

Everyone tried their best attacks. There was ice as they attempted to freeze the Devourer, mist as Violet tried to confuse him, then electric blasts and more—an onslaught of every power they had.

And still the Devourer laughed, and his eyes glowed ever brighter, and Lance knew they were making him stronger. Each attack only fed him.

Would there be any way to defeat him? Lance felt desperate. He knew that once they stopped battling the Devourer, after he stopped feeding on the power of their attacks, he would move to swallowing them whole.

And Lance could not let that happen. He had one more idea.

Infinity, I need you to channel your golden elixir into me, thought Lance. *Like how we defeated the Swarm!*

I worry it will not work, Infinity replied.

We have to try. Lance felt no fear; he was beyond fear. All he felt was a fierce protectiveness—he would protect the Dragon Force, he would protect Zoe, he would protect his friends and all of the New World. He would do whatever it took.

Infinity began to glow with the power of golden elixir. Lance felt the power course through him, and then suddenly he was glowing as well.

He took out his erhu and began to play more fiercely than he ever had. It was a desperate, furious song. He poured what was left of his strength into it. He put every last drop of himself into this song, and it flowed out of him. All around him the rest of the Dragon Force seemed to be blown back by the power of it. But Lance barely noticed them, all of his focus and attention on his playing, and on the Devourer himself.

Infinity flew straight at the Devourer, and Lance prepared for anything—he prepared for him to swallow him and he prepared for him to swipe at him, to attack him with a thousand Petrifiers.

But instead the Devourer simply watched him and

Infinity. And then he began to inhale, and Lance felt the very magic that was inside him get sucked out. It felt as if he couldn't breathe, as if air was getting drawn out of him, and he felt the magic he had gained with Infinity and their shared golden elixir pour out of his mouth and eyes and ears and his very pores.

He was going to be a husk.

Infinity let out a whimper and then dived away from the Devourer, but even that hurt. Lance felt his magic getting pulled out of him.

"LANCE! LET GO!" Infinity cried. The command was so loud and startling and insistent that Lance did what she asked, and he tumbled off her back and landed on the floor of the den below.

Then Infinity flew right up to the Devourer's great gaping maw. She glowed and glowed, light flowing out of her and toward the Devourer, and he drank it all. She spun away from the Devourer, so they were no longer facing him. Her horns glowed even brighter, and a bubble, much like the one she had summoned when she and Lance were about to be swallowed by the shark-dragon, appeared around her. Lance wondered if the bubble was even impenetrable to the Devourer.

"It is me you want," Infinity said, and her voice broke. "This must be what was prophesized. I make golden elixir. I make the magic that you crave. If you take me, you will have an endless source of magic and power."

"INFINITY! NO!" screamed Lance. He leaped up into the air, trying to fly to her, but the bubble she had made kept him out. He couldn't even hear her down their bond. She was closed off to him, and it hurt, oh it hurt, and she was his dragon and he would not—could not—let her do this. There had to be another way. He jumped up again but he could not get to her.

"Why would I not devour this world, and all in it, and take you as well?" said the Devourer. But Lance could tell he was curious, that he was considering Infinity's offer.

"This world has such little true magic," said Infinity. "It would taste sour to you—one who has tasted so much of what the cosmos has to offer. And I will only come with you willingly if you leave the

New World alone. And then I will pour all my own energy into only making as much golden elixir as you crave."

"I am always hungry," said the Devourer. "Golden elixir is not enough for me."

Infinity bared her teeth. "You have never tasted pure golden elixir. See for yourself."

A stream of golden magic seeped through the bubble, and the Devourer lapped it up, and then paused. "You are right—even one sip of that has more power in it than some entire planets I have devoured."

The Devourer took a long sniff, as if he were smelling all of the world.

"The golden dragon is right. This is a broken world, and I do not want it. I will take the Infinite Dragon instead."

He turned his snout to Infinity. "Promise me that you will be my unlimited power source."

Infinity hung her head.

"NO! Don't do it!" Lance was crying now, tears flooding down his cheeks.

Infinity glanced at him. "Thank you, Lance. Being

your dragon has been everything I'd ever hoped for. But this is what was prophesised. This is what was meant to happen. This is how I save everyone." A single golden tear fell from her eye. "I will do it. I will go with you, and I will make you golden elixir if you promise to leave the New World, and everyone in it. Then I will go with you."

"Done," said the Devourer. And then there was a whirring around them all, like a sudden hurricane. "But I will take the magic from this world with me. It is not natural, after all, for humans to have magic."

"That was not the offer!" cried Infinity, but it was too late—she was bound by her word. Even in his grief at seeing his dragon sacrifice herself, Lance realized that she had not been precise enough in her demands, that the Devourer was leaving the New World as promised, but not before draining it of all magic. Then the Devourer reached out and gripped Infinity in his massive claws, and she went limp.

"INFINITY!" Lance felt as if his heart was shattering into a million pieces, as if he was losing a part of himself, as if he would be left with a gaping hole that could never be filled. He was screaming and crying and still he tried to get to her, still he tried to save his dragon. But the magic from golden elixir in his suit was disappearing, and he could not hover.

The Devourer snarled at everyone in the den. "Consider yourselves lucky that I have let you live." The Devourer inhaled again, and Lance could see all the magic from the humans, and even the dragons, flowing out of them and into the Devourer's gaping maw. He felt what was left of his magic get sucked out of him, and it hurt. But not as much as the pain of seeing Infinity go limp.

A trick—the Devourer had tricked them.

Then the Devourer lifted another paw, clawed a hole in the sky beyond, and disappeared through it, taking Infinity with him.

Infinite Hope

Lance found himself in a state of shock. All he could hear was a distant buzzing. He kept trying to talk to Infinity through their bond, but he couldn't hear her.

And then he felt a sudden, indescribable pain that shot through his heart, and he let out a cry and collapsed.

Zoe flew to him, still a dragon, nudging him with her nose. He was aware she was saying something, but he couldn't hear it—all he could hear was the Devourer's laugh as he took the magic, and took Infinity. It felt as if something was pulling on his heart, pulling so hard that he thought it might burst out of his chest.

And then there was a sudden release, like an uncoiled spring coming back together.

That was somehow worse. He knew, instinctively, that the intense pain came from being separated from Infinity and it was because the Devourer had taken her somewhere far across the cosmos. Somewhere Lance and the others could never follow. And when the release had come, Lance wondered if it meant that his connection to Infinity had been snapped.

The bond never breaks, said a voice, loud and clear and insistent enough to cut through the haze surrounding Lance. He sat up and rubbed his eyes.

Billy Chan and his dragon, Spark, were right there with him, and Spark was staring at him with her golden eyes. She spoke again. "The bond never breaks. Only death can break the dragon-human heart-bond. No matter where the Devourer takes Infinity, you will still be bonded to her."

"How do you know?" Lance's voice shook.

Billy put his hand on Spark. "We once were separated across realms. Spark closed herself to me, but still the bond was there. It cannot break. And we will find her, Lance." Billy raised his voice so that it echoed around the den. "We may have lost our magic, but we have not lost our purpose, nor our heart. We are still the Dragon Force, and we will fight for what is right, and to defend the New World."

Above him, over the ripped open roof of the den, the hole that the Devourer had gone through gaped like a hungry mouth. It wasn't like a portal; it was a rip in the sky, and Lance didn't want to think about what might come through it next.

Lance forced himself to stand. Everything hurt. Arthur and Bea ran over and threw their arms around him. "I'm so sorry, Lance," said Bea.

"We're going to get her back," added Arthur, his voice fierce. "Nobody takes our dragons!"

Jaws, who was right behind them, growled in agreement. "Arthur is right—we will find Infinity."

Violet flew over, flapping her wings furiously, but no mist came. "My healing mist is gone," she said. "I am sorry, Lance. I hoped to help heal you." She breathed out experimentally, and a small burst of flames came. "At least I can still breathe fire."

Next to him, Zoe sputtered and snorted, and

Lance knew she was trying to breathe fire too. But nothing happened. "Why can't I breathe fire too?"

"Because you are not a true dragon," said Violet gently. "Your magic came from golden elixir."

"Then why am I still a dragon?" Zoe demanded. "If all the magic is gone, shouldn't I have turned back into a human?"

"This may mean the dragon is your permanent form now," said Violet. "We did warn you of that."

Zoe's dragon eyes widened. "But I can't breathe fire now! I'm not a real dragon at all! I'm just trapped in a dragon body." Her voice wobbled, as if she was about to cry.

And Lance knew that he had to be brave. He had to fight the pain and sorrow of being separated from Infinity. He had to be brave for Zoe. For Infinity. For the Dragon Force. For himself.

He could not wallow in his self-pity and sadness because Infinity was gone.

Because he was going to get her back. But to do that, he needed to be stronger than he'd ever been. He knew that. But he also knew he wouldn't have to do it alone, and that gave him strength.

He put his arm around his dragon sister. "It's okay, Zoe," he said. "We are going to figure it out. I'm here. And Violet is here. We're all here." His voice cracked. "Well, we're almost all here." He looked to the hole in the sky, and even though he couldn't feel Infinity through their bond, he sent a burst of hope through their bond, just in case she might feel it, wherever she was. And she would know that he wasn't going to give up on her.

The hole in the sky above them began to shimmer.

"Dragon Force, get together!" yelled Billy, and the group all gathered close, watching the shimmering hole with trepidation. "I know our magic and powers are gone, but our true magic has always been the bonds we share, and the strength of our friendship."

Four dragons soared through. Four dragons that looked strangely familiar to Lance in a way he could not figure out. Light glinted within their bodies, refracting and reflecting. Their wings looked like sheets of cut glass, and each one was a different color. Diamond white, emerald green, ruby red, and sapphire blue. They looked as if they had been cut from gemstones and brought to life.

Next to Lance, Billy gasped.

"Your magic may be gone, but ours is not," said the diamond-white dragon.

"We have been waiting a long time to come home," said the emerald-green one. "We were trapped outside this universe, but that hole has allowed us to come back in."

"However, be warned, there are other things outside this universe that should not come in, and now will be able to," added the sapphire dragon. "We know that Infinity has been taken." The dragon glared at Billy. "We left her in your care, Billy Chan." Billy gulped and hung his head.

"I'm sorry," he said. "She sacrificed herself—we couldn't stop her."

"This is not her destiny," said the diamond-white dragon in a low growl.

"Who are you?" Lance burst out. The gemstone dragons all looked at him with their fiery eyes.

"You are Infinity's human," said the ruby-red dragon. "I can tell. We are the Diamond Clan. And we will help you find Infinity. She was once entrusted to us, and we have never stopped caring about her. She cannot be lost."

Lance remembered the story that Infinity had told—about the Diamond Clan, and how they had raised her as a hatchling. They had come back, for Infinity. They had come back, and they still had their magic.

He looked at the four magnificent gemstone dragons—dragons unlike any he had ever seen. Dragons who were linked to Infinity. "We'll find Infinity," he said, his voice strong. They would find Infinity, they would bring back the magic, and they would defeat the Devourer once and for all.

The four gemstone dragons appraised Lance. "It will be hard," said the ruby dragon. "But it is not impossible. You must not give up hope."

"Never," Lance whispered, as he felt hope take root inside his heart. *Infinity*, he thought. *Infinity, we're coming.*

Acknowledgments

Thank you to our readers for continuing the dragon adventure with us! We hope you loved *Devourer's Attack*.

We feel so lucky to be able to create these characters and this world, and we love writing these books. We have so many people to thank who make the books a reality!

We would like to thank our amazing agent, Claire Wilson, for always leading us in the right direction and continuously believing in us. Thank you as well to Sam Coates at RCW for sending our dragons all over the world, Safae El-Ouahabi for her support, and Emily Hayward-Whitlock at the Artist's Partnership.

Thank you, as always, to the incomparable Rachel Denwood at Simon & Schuster Children's Books. This book is dedicated to Rachel, and these books would not exist without her. What an adventure it has been—we are so lucky to be able to work with you. Long last our author-editor adventures!

We would also like to thank the amazing Amina Youssef who worked on three of the Dragon Realm books and the first two Dragon Force books. Thank you for everything—we will miss working with you so much! You will always be Team Dragon to us.

And a big thank-you and welcome to Michelle Misra who has just joined Team Dragon! Thank you for helping us polish up *Devourer's Attack*—we are very excited to work with you on the next book!

We would also like to thank the rest of the wonderful team at Simon & Schuster. Laura Hough, sales wizard! Dan Fricker, the marketing champion! Ellen Abernethy, PR superstar! Jesse Green, design queen! Truly, the best team any authors could ask for.

Our main author diva demand is that we always request to have Catherine Coe do the copy edit because she is just the best. Catherine, thank you for knowing our world as well as we do, for always understanding our jokes, and catching our many, many repetitive phrases.

And how lucky are we to have another stunning cover? We are so happy that we get to continue to work with illustrator extraordinaire, Petur Antonsson. Petur, thank you for bringing our dragons to life so beautifully. Your illustrations are perfect.

A huge thank-you to all the booksellers, teachers, and librarians for championing our dragon books. We'd like to especially thank Sanchita and the team at the Children's Bookshop, Muswell Hill, LJ Ireton at Waterstones Finchley Road, and Rhiannon Tripp at Waterstones High Street Kensington. We'd also like to thank Waterstones for their ongoing support.

We are so grateful to our own wonderful dragon clan for their support and love—thank you especially to Jack, Cat, Jane, Stephanie, Ben P, Tom, Kiran, Anna, Kate, Samantha, Krystal, Jeni, Maarten, Dyna, Kris, KWoo, Rosi, and Ben O for being such bright lights in our lives. And a special shout-out to some of our favorite little dragons—Cooper, Matilde, Lyra, Mylo, Lark, Rose, and Coral.

Of course our biggest thanks goes to our parents for everything they've done for us. A special thank-you to Kevin's parents, Paulus and Louisa, for coming to the Dragon Force launch and helping with child care so we could actually write the book! And to our own daughters, Evie and Mira—you make every day better, and we love you so much. We can't wait to share these books with you.

KATIE & KEVIN TSANG met in 2008 while studying at the Chinese University of Hong Kong. Since then they have lived on three different continents and traveled to over forty countries together. As well as the Dragon Realm and Dragon Force series, they are the cowriters of the young fiction series Sam Wu Is Not Afraid (Egmont) and Space Blasters (Farshore) and Katie also writes young adult as Katherine Webber.

Turn the page to read
the next installment of

DRAGON FORCE

Coming soon!

Dragon's Claw had closed itself.

The claws were curled up in a fist, and the entire peninsula impossible to access.

Only the lagoons were left—the Deep Dark, the Water Jungle, and the Mirage. But without the claws around them, they looked odd. And all the shine and magic that once coursed through them was gone.

Lance had seen it happen once before, when the attacks on Camp Claw had first happened. Lance hoped that now it meant that the magic inside Dragon's Claw was somehow still protected. That Dragon's Claw could be restored once more.

If Infinity were here, she would have been able

to sense what was happening. She would have even been able to open an entrance to Dragon's Claw, because of her connection with the very essence and magic of the Claw itself.

But Infinity wasn't here. She had been taken by the Devourer, and was so far away that Lance could feel the unbreakable bond between them stretching beyond its limits.

It hadn't broken yet, though, and that gave him hope.

As did, strangely, the sight of the Claw balled up in a fist. Still fighting.

"Where do we go?" he said to Billy Chan. Since his own dragon was gone, Lance was sitting astride Spark, Billy's dragon.

Once, the very idea that he would be riding alongside the leader of Dragon Force on his legendary dragon would have been the most incredible thing that Lance could have ever imagined.

But now he was numb to it. Because the only reason he was riding Spark was because his dragon, his Infinity, was gone.

Billy was silent for a moment.

Lance knew that Billy and Spark were communicating through their bond, and in that moment he hated Billy and Spark, hated everyone who still had their dragon.

He would have given anything to be able to communicate with Infinity.

"We will go to Dracordia," said a voice beside them. The voice of the Diamond Dragon, one of the gemstone dragons who had appeared after Infinity had been taken. The Diamond Clan, named for the Diamond dragon itself, were unlike any dragons Lance had ever seen or heard about. They appeared to be carved from gems themselves, and they had been the dragons who had raised Infinity, who had protected her after her own mother had died.

And then they had disappeared, and returned to the New World through the hole that the Devourer had ripped in the sky.

The Diamond Dragon cocked its head to the side now, assessing Lance. "Lance Lo, I have never heart-bonded with a human. And I have never even allowed a human to ride me. But I know you are

Infinity's human. So for that reason, and that reason alone, I invite you to sit astride me."

Lance gulped. Riding a dragon that you weren't heart-bonded to was risky. Without the bond, it was easy to fall off.

And the Diamond Dragon looked especially lethal to sit on, all jagged edges that could slice through a person.

But Lance knew what an honor it was to be asked. He met the Diamond Dragon's fiery gaze.

"Thank you," he said. "That is very generous of you."

"Do not make me regret the offer," retorted the Diamond Dragon. "Quickly now. We must seek out the safe place in Dracordia before other dragons find it." The Diamond Dragon flew closer to Spark.

Still in midair, Lance carefully slid off of Spark's back and landed with a thump on the Diamond Dragon's back.

Its hard exterior was extremely uncomfortable. "May I hold on?" he asked.

The Diamond Dragon snorted. "Of course. How else will you stay on?"

Lance carefully wrapped his arms around the

Diamond Dragon's neck. And then he gasped as the dragon shifted its scales, and it was suddenly malleable, like gold melting.

"That will make holding on more comfortable," said the Diamond Dragon.

"What... what should I call you?" asked Lance. A dragon's name was a very personal thing—and when a human and a dragon heart-bonded, the human would choose a new name for them, one that they would be called for as long as that human lived. All dragons had original names, of course, but the heart-bonded human name was meant to represent who they were.

"Diamond will do," said Diamond. "You may call all four of us by our gemstones." Diamond glanced back at the rest of her clan. The bright-red Ruby dragon, the shimmering blue Sapphire, and the shining green Emerald.

"Lance, you are very lucky to be invited to ride on Diamond." Billy's voice was solemn. "And Diamond, all of Dragon Force thank you and your clan for joining us in our mission to find Infinity and defeat the Devourer."

"Do not mistake our motives," said Diamond. "We care for Infinity. She must be found. This does not make us part of your little group."

Spark's eyes flashed at the insult.

"That only makes me all the more grateful for your help," said Billy. "And you know that we are just as desperate to find Infinity as you are."

"No. Only the boy, Lance Lo, cares as much as we do," said Diamond. "Which is why I allow him to ride on me."

She sighed. "Dracordia is where we must go, but it will be dangerous. Dragons will be enraged at their magic being stolen, and they will blame humans."

"At least we've got you on our side," said Lance. "And you still have your magic."

Because the Diamond Clan had arrived after the Devourer had disappeared, taking Infinity and all the magic in the New World with him, they still had their dragon magic.

"Indeed," said Diamond. "But that will make any dragons we come across even more wary and distrustful of us."

"Other dragons are the least of our worries," said

Ruby, beginning to flap her great wings. "It appears we have some unwelcome visitors."

Lance looked up just in time to see what appeared to be a balled-up spider fall from the hole in the sky, and then the creature exploded.

The blast sent all of Dragon Force pinwheeling and spinning in different directions, and from the cries, Lance suspected several Dragon Force members had been struck.

With his ears ringing, Lance desperately looked around the sky for his sister, Zoe. She was still stuck in dragon form, and she wasn't a strong flier.

As he searched for her, he saw something that made his skin crawl.

The exploding spider creature was beginning to re-form. It had blasted itself out but was now coming back together. Bigger than before.

And Lance knew it was preparing for another blast . . .